— Before I Wake —

and

Other Tales

by Detroiters

— Before I Wake —

and

Other Tales

by Detroiters

* * *

**Detroit Black Writers' Guild
1990**

© 1990 Detroit Black Writers' Guild, Inc.
Second Printing April 1994

All Rights Reserved

ISBN: 0961-3078-70

Library of Congress Catalog Card Number:
91-70953

Dedication

*This book is dedicated to:
Peggy A. Moore in recognition
of her perseverance, determination,
and committment to public service.*

Thank you, Peggy.

Black Writers' Guild
member and friends

"The struggle is my life."
— *Nelson Mandela '90*

Acknowledgements

Patricia Morris - Editor

Lafayette King - Editor and Word Processor

Sandra Miller - Word Processor

Herbert R. Metoyer, Jr. - Senior Editor and Word Processor

Peggy A. Moore - Director, Project Coordinator and Managing Editor

* * *

CONTENTS

#	Title	Author	Page
	Foreword		9
1.	Street Dancer	Jones	11
2.	Fire of Spring	Nance	16
3.	The Encounter	Moore	23
4.	The Awakening of Hanna Lee	Metoyer	29
5.	Images	Hunter	46
6.	A Father for Malik	Morris	49
7.	Melody Unchained	Suma	56
8.	The Greenfields	Jones	64
9.	Winter Reprieve	King	67
10.	He Was Magnificent	Lewis	79
11.	A Fantasy	Green	81
12.	Judgment Day on South Street	Metoyer	90
13.	Letter to William	Moore	99
14.	Before I Wake	Nance	110
15.	The Washtenaw Incident	Tolliver	115
16.	Peeping Jane	Hunter	130
17.	Lance Courage	Anderson	138
18.	Hard Times	Metoyer	147
	Authors' Biographies		155

Foreword

The Black Writers' Guild was founded in 1983 as a non-profit organization for the specific purpose of increasing literacy awareness and to encourage inner city residents (young and old) to write as an alternative to the many less positive activities available within the city. Our first project was a book of poetry we entitled, *Through Ebony Eyes* (1986).

This publication, *Before I Awake,* a book of selected short stories, was published by the Guild in order to give our writers an opportunity to see something of theirs in print and, hopefully, to encourage them to continue in this very rewarding field.

Before I Awake, then, was not intended to be a literary or commercial masterpiece, but a training vehicle through which we can measure our progress and growth over the years through subsequent publications.

Some of our writers have made astounding progress and, while we salute these, we cannot ignore the hard work of our beginners — those who are struggling to help fill the wide gap left by the ravages of time over the past four-hundred years. To them, we offer a very special salute.

While the primary goal of the Guild is to foster literature slanted toward capturing and recording *black experiences*, member ship is open to any and all persons with similar interests, for it is through wholesome relationships such as this that we can all learn — and grow.

Your purchase of this book is appreciated. All monies earned go toward the support of this especially noteworthy project.

Peggy A. Moore
Founder & Director

Herbert R. Metoyer
Senior Editor

Street Dancer

by
Robert Kenyatta Jones

When Bennie woke up that morning, the Specklebird was nowhere to be found. He was not on the windowsill where he sometimes sat, nor was he in the woodshed, skulking about the sawdust floor. And there was no sign of him amid the ripening corn.

Bennie had been aware for some time now, that the Specklebird's visits were becoming less frequent, but he would almost always pop up in the corn field. And it did not matter when. It could be in late November as he crunched across the hard, snow-patched furrows, stopping here and there to kick at some crusty stalks left over from the Halloween teepees. But it was August now, and early. The corn was heavy with dew. It was quiet. There was no wind. Altogether, it was a perfect setting for one of the Specklebird's visits, but he would not show up. Bennie wasn't worried though, about the Specklebird's absence. He was occupied with something else. He was thinking about the street dance to be held that evening.

From the time he arose, he had looked forward to the street dance. He had been to street dances before, but he knew, somehow, that this one would be different. He knew the procedure. They would close off Chippewa Street, in front of the school, from Indiana to Wisconsin streets. Then, they would erect a stage where only the best dancers would perform and where the dance contest would be held. The rest would dance in the street. But not him. He and his pals would romp across the school lawn, darting in and out of the hedges, and then hide in the tall, bushy shrubbery. They would play "Snap-the-Rope" and other games, tease both the girls and dancers, and then dash off to hide again. It would be the same he thought. The same — but different.

He fidgeted, pacing back and forth through the kitchen, opening and closing the ice box. He did annoying things until he finally stepped on his mother's last nerve. "Boy," she shouted, "get out of this house and go find yourself something to do."

With that, he went over to the green fields where he stretched out on the summer grass. He lay motionless, with eyes closed, listening to the hypnotic drone of a single distant airplane. The day was still and he became still; certain in his uncertainty and comfortable in his ignorance. He dozed.

The warmth of the noon sun had left him and he opened his eyes to low gray clouds where the sun had been. It began to rain. It was one of those summer rains, short-lived, with no thunder. The kind of rain when, at other times, he would have stuck a straight pin into the ground and listened to see if the devil really was *beating his wife*. This myth and the thunderless summer storm, however, held no appeal for him now. So, he sprinted for home, deeply concerned that the street dance would be cancelled. He arrived home, and changed into dry clothing and watched the rain.

The day dragged on. Even when the rain stopped, and he was secure in his knowledge that the street dance would not be cancelled, the day dragged on. It seemed to hang suspended between one o'clock and forever. The oatmeal cookies, hot from the oven, could not add one second to the sun's pace. He was like the blind dog in a meat house, sniffing everywhere, content nowhere.

With tedious decorum, the sun sank into gray clouds. The sky flushed and darkened, and the evening star flickered into sight. Now he was aglow, buoyant, a skilled athlete, honed and ready for the race. Evening was upon him. An evening, soaked by an afternoon rain and warmed by its own low sun, now engulfed him in false permanence. The sounds around him, though tumbling through pitch and tone, seemed fixed in slow progression as they rolled under the baton, held loosely, by a musician called "Summer." Night came; and with it, the street dance.

* * *

They were playing "Red Rover," and all of his earlier thoughts had been lost or covered by the joy of the game. Until now. She had brushed against him while attempting to break through the human chain. He had been bumped, and pushed, and even knocked down before. But this time he was brushed by her. An odd shove, firm yet soft, but lacking the object frenzy of "Red Rover." The thought that it was a careless encounter, an accident, was crushed when she bumped him again. He felt a new sensation, something both scary and fine. It rose from the pit of his stomach, dull at first, then bright and went straight to his head. An instant of indescribable beauty held him breathless as his body responded to a feeling, many feelings, each charged with a vague delight, swelling and falling in mysterious intensities. His mind was reeling and he fought to understand what was happening to him. An odd warmth bubbled across his once cool limbs. She brushed him again. Now he sought her out, encouraging the opportunity for her soft breasts to graze his chest and hands. He was delirious, a ragged, airy creature floating between deliberation and desire.

* * *

The street dance was over and the warm August night had burned itself out. He lay in the midst of the tall, thick grasses which separated the rhubarb patch from the alley. It was cool now, and yet, he sweated. He could no longer separate the horse and rider that bore down upon him from the swirling heavens. Polaris winked at him and shifted from side to side, while steady Cassiopeia was having a difficult time deciding whether to be a "W" or an "M."

As he lay in confusion, a dull, dim fragment of his past slowly merged with his sharp, bright present. Try as he would, he could not repress this frightening fragment. He could see it clearly, as though it happened that morning. It was four years ago. He was ten. She had called to him and he had come to her. She was a woman, full and smelling beyond his senses. He had always said ma'am to her. She offered him money to come into the house. They were alone. She told him to wait, and he had waited. She went into the bedroom, then called him in, and he went in. She was in the bed. "Climb up here Bennie," she had said. He said "Yes, ma'am," and he did as he was told. He climbed onto the bed. "Before I give you this money, you've got to promise me you won't tell anybody. Promise?" she asked, and he promised. She pulled back the patchwork quilt and exposed her bare body from her breasts to just below her navel. He stiffened with fright.

"Don't be afraid Bennie," she said forming a warm smile. "I'm not going to hurt you."

Slowly, she took his trembling hand and placed it on her breast. She began massaging both breasts with his stiff, unresponsive hand. A stiffness overcame his whole body as she pulled him over and on top of her. "Sweetheart, sweetheart," she moaned. He was confused. When she tried to roll over on top of him her firm grip loosened. He recoiled in explicable fear and sprang away, jumping from the bed. He did not run until he heard her say "Come back." He flew. Her words grew faint very fast. "Come back! Don't tell! Come back! Don't tell." Later, he realized he had forgot the money. He dare not go back. He did keep his promise. He did not tell anyone. That was when the Specklebird first appeared. He had come cooing in, bright, friendly, and dependable. Until now.

    Bennie lay still and squeezed his eyes shut tight as if this action would help him reconcile his opposing emotions of his past and present. It did not. He could not. Now, he yearned for the Specklebird. He would tell him everything. And the Specklebird would explain it all. Of this he was certain. The Specklebird knew things. Not like the grownups. The grownups knew everything, but the Specklebird knew special things. The Specklebird would speak to him about things not being the same or what they seemed to be. About old summers and strange winters. It was not that he understood everything that the Specklebird had to say. It was more the comfort and the trust that came from the soothing songs the Specklebird would sing — strange, attractive, haunting song. A song of strength, a song of faith, a song that said "hold on." But the Specklebird had flown, and he was forced to concede alone that he could no longer play on the lawn.

* * *

The Fire of Spring

by
Michael Nance

He sat dreaming, staring at the pale blue sky through the cracked window, his thoughts drifting back to a one-room schoolhouse in southern Georgia. *With spring came the lilacs.* . . . He had walked ten miles back and forth to the dilapidated school, past three white schools.

Miss Brown taught all eight grades at the Booker T. Washington school. She was an attractive, brown-skinned woman of middle age with a withered left hand. She reminded the children constantly that black people had a glorious history. She told them of the regal pomp of Songhay, the splendor of Timbuktu, Egypt with its Gods and pyramids, the Moors, Dubois and Frederick Douglass, and the paintings of Tanner. She was a remarkable woman who, like most of her students, came out of a poor sharecropper's cabin. Despite this, she had managed to acquire a college degree with honors.

School lasted only three months a year, for the children had to work the cotton fields from "can't see" in the morning until "can't see" at night from planting to harvest. The rest of the year, they worked for Mr. Stern, a farmer of German extraction, who then, in the '30s, had a great admiration for his fellow countryman, Adolph Hitler. Stern was also reputed to belong to the hierarchy of an organization called the "Khristian Knights."

When he graduated from Miss Brown's school, he and his father, who was illiterate, had a serious talk. "You got you a good learnin'," his father had said. "Me

— I had to work for Mr. *Chuck* all my life. Now you gots to hep me an yer ma."

So, he reflected on the situation, coming to the conclusion at fourteen, that it was time he left Georgia and went North to complete his education — there being not much future for a black boy in the cotton fields of Georgia in 1936.

He came to Detroit by rail, hopped a train, and lied about his age which was easy since he was, at fourteen, over six feet tall and already sporting a thin mustache. By day, he worked as a bus boy, and finished high school at Northern High by going to school at night.

Although he was bright and had done well in night school, college was out of the question. So, after he got his diploma, he went to work at the huge, sprawling Ford Rouge complex. He was then almost nineteen years old, having vague aspirations, fostered by Miss Brown, of becoming a "Race Man" and helping his people.

To his disappointment, the Ford Rouge plant proved to be a continuation of the plantation system that he had sought to leave behind in the South. After working there for a few months, he awoke one Sunday morning to hear something about a *Day Of Infamy* — The Japanese had bombed Pearl Harbor and the United States entered World War II.

Out of some vague, unfounded feeling of patriotism, coupled with his spirit of adventure, he enlisted the next week. Much of the next three years was spent on the sands of North Africa fighting Rommel, trudging through the burning sands, his throat parched, his eyes melting under the burning glare of the African sun. He encountered many dangers, but at the end, he came out of it a hero with three medals to attest to his bravery.

Back in Detroit, he returned to the dull grind of the factory.

One day, he read some protest literature passed out by some radicals in the plant. The literature impressed him. It put into words many of the vague ideas that he had developed over the years. He had always been something of a militant. Miss Brown had instilled in him a deep racial pride. As a result, he had never been ashamed of what he was, and had always been a proud black man, even under the harshest type of racial oppression.

The literature dealt with racism, but it went farther than that. It talked about how the working class was oppressed by a greedy minority of wealthy men with their minions and lackeys, and how black workers suffered under a dual type of oppression — class and race. It made a lot of sense to him. It articulated feelings hitherto repressed or perhaps overlooked.

He began talking to some of these radicals. From them, he learned a lot about other proud, brilliant black radicals like Paul Robeson and W.E.B. Dubois. He read their writings along with those of Marx, Engels, Lenin, Stalin, and others, and he began to think of his destiny and the destiny of other struggling blacks.

It was about this time that he met Carol. She was a beautiful, black intellectual who was studying for her Ph.D. and who had become involved in the radical movement. She took an interest in him because she saw that he had a good mind, *albeit somewhat untrained*, and took it upon herself to help him develop it. What started out as friendship on an intellectual level eventually blossomed into love.

He had known all kinds of women, young girls amid the cotton flowers in Georgia, prostitutes in Europe and North Africa, fast women on the streets of Detroit, white women in radical circles, but never a woman like Carol. She was sincere, and loving, and she respected him for what he was. And for the first time in his life, he felt happy and fulfilled.

Then, tragedy struck. Carol went to hear Paul Robeson speak at Peekskill, New York. She went alone because he was hospitalized with appendicitis at the time and could not go. She was among many brutally beaten by the racist, reactionary hordes that descended upon the freedom fighters, while racist cops looked on, cheering like animals. A wild-eyed, white thug ripped off Carol's blouse, then beat her in the head with a piece of concrete.

He was heartsick when he heard about Peekskill and Carol's tragedy. They brought her back, a vegetable, to a hospital outside of Detroit. He had visited her often, but all she could do was stare vacantly into space. Sometime later, she died of a brain hemorrhage.

Her death reminded him of a lynching he had witnessed from behind a clump of bushes as a boy that echoed Lady Day's "Strange Fruit." He had written, sometime earlier, in his notebook: Whenever I hear Billie Holiday's "Strange Fruit," I close my eyes and behold a vision of utter horror — a black man of middle age, very dark complexioned, hanging from the bough of a poplar tree. He wears a white shirt, drenched with blood, as is his head. A steady stream of dark blood drips from his crotch while those below him dance the dance of jinn — *Strange fruit hanging from the poplar trees.*

Lynchers had no respect for sex . . . they *lynched* Carol.

He had been deeply in love with her, they had shared so much, and it took him a while to put his life back together.

* * *

One night, he saw, coming out of a bar on Oakland Avenue, a jovial-looking, rotund figure who he recognized immediately as the famous bebop musician, Charlie Parker. Bird was dressed somewhat haphazardly and walking swiftly.

Suddenly Bird stopped and stared curiously at him for a moment before walking off down the street toward a questionable house. Being an avid fan of new music, many times he sat in his empty room, listening again and again to records of Bird playing "Embraceable You," "Out of Nowhere," or "My Old Flame." He liked Bird's ballads best.

He had pondered over Bird's life, wondering — how could a man live with so much pain and tragedy, and still have so much beauty in his soul?

He had heard, from a friend in New York who knew Bird, that Bird often quoted a passage from Omar Khayyám's Rubáiyát. Could it be that this passage held the essence of what Bird was? Until the day he died, he would always remember that night.

A short time later, he was summoned before a band of racist, reactionary hypocrites known as the House Un-American Activities Committee, allegedly, for his "subversive" actions. These, of course, consisted of fighting for the rights of all oppressed people against an unjust system.

He conducted himself with great dignity and courage during these proceedings, answering the onslaughts of these reprobates with candor and wit.

Shortly after this, however, he lost his job and was ostracized from the community due to the efforts of certain self-serving "leaders" who sought to use the McCarthy era to bootlick their way to influence and material gain.

Still, he remained active in the movement, spending much time writing — refusing to be discouraged.

Recurring stomach pains led him, after a period of procrastination, to visit the doctor. His worst fears were realized. He was dying of cancer.

Now, while he sat in his small, clean room, looking out his cracked window, and reflecting on death, he wrote:

How shall I die
Writhing painfully
Upon my dreary deathbed
or in a peaceful slumber
It matters not, for when I am gone
The snow will still melt in early Spring
And the trees will still shed Autumn leaves
Children will still laugh
And birds will not stop singing
Men will continue to be born
And live and die
And love and hate and kill and multiply
Grass will remain green
The sky blue
Music will be played
Songs sung
Words written
Spoken
Love made
And man made to feel unbearable agony
For I am but an infinitesimal speck
In the expanse of eternity

With those words written, he lay aside his pen and spent this — his last Spring, in bittersweet dreaming.

Carol was gone forever, no more than a beautiful, fleeting memory. Ma and Pa were long since gone, buried beneath the red Georgia clay. Miss Brown? Perhaps she was still around, and perhaps other bright, young black men would hear her message as he had.

The smell of lilacs wafted in the breeze. Life, he thought, was sweet — *like the lilacs* . . . .

* * *

The Encounter

by
Peggy A. Moore

The dusty old pickup truck slowed as it turned apprehensively onto a dead-end street of a Black Detroit neighborhood. Splattered mud nearly covered the dented license plate on the back of the vehicle, making the six-digit number difficult to read. The two occupants, both white, twenty-year-old, sandy-haired Randy, and seventeen-year-old blond-haired Karen, began looking to the right and left as their dilapidated truck coasted to five miles per hour. They were searching for a black gal named Tanya who was supposed to be dressed in a neon-colored, spandex jumpsuit. Their friends had told them that Tanya would spot them long before they saw her — it always happened that way. Nevertheless, they continued to scan the empty block.

Finally, Randy steered the battered pickup to the curb, applied the brakes, and turned the ignition off. Then, the two of them sat in silence, waiting and watching. Karen moved closer to Randy and rested her head gently on his shoulder.

Karen's father owned a chicken farm and egg hatchery about thirty miles outside of Detroit near Wixom. Randy worked for her father during the summer months and used his earnings to further his college education. Both had known each other for most of their lives, but had only just recently began dating each other. They had driven into Detroit looking for some kind of excitement — something their rural home failed to offer.

Earlier, as they took the exit off the I-94 freeway,

they noticed immediately, that there was an increase in the number of huge billboards which suggestively proclaimed the powers of beer, whiskey, and cigarettes. The gaudy urban ads were everywhere and seemed to dominate the entire skyline that led into Detroit.

Karen had never ventured this deep into a Detroit neighborhood before, but she'd read many stories about its horrors in the daily papers — about how visiting a Detroit neighborhood was like being on the set of a wild west "shoot'em up."

Slowly, Karen lifted her head from Randy's shoulder and glanced out of the window. What she saw was a lot different from what she had read or heard. She noted that the few houses remaining on this particular block had massive rolling spaces of manicured lawns between them, coupled with a backdrop of blue Colorado spruce and pine trees — much like her own area near Wixom. She theorized that the acres upon acres of vacant land was probably the result of the extensive federal program she had heard about which used the National Guard to tear down much of the old housing stock. Apparently, they had done a good job.

Straining her eyes to look out across a field of wild flowers, Karen caught a quick glimpse of a brown rabbit nibbling in the grass, and above him, like some woodland sentry, a tiny squirrel perched precariously on the slender limb of a tree. She smiled, wondering to herself if this was how Detroit looked at the turn of the century.

Suddenly, as if from nowhere, Tanya appeared, peering at them through the dirty windshield of the pickup truck — standing tall and erect like an urban goddess. To Randy, Tanya looked just as his friends had described her — stately, smooth, jet-black, and beautiful.

Very quickly, Tanya gave Randy and Karen the once-over, blinking her long-lashed eyes, as if waiting for her keen perception to determine if Randy and Karen were okay. When she was satisfied, Tanya reached for the rusty handle and opened the door. Randy smiled as his eyes were drawn to her silky-smooth hand adorned with highly lacquered nails painted with the color of morning marigolds.

Tanya motioned to Karen to move over as she climbed in and settled in the front seat on her cushiony hips causing Randy to release a deep sigh as he stared transfixed at this "black beauty." A woman, who was rumored to be one of the richest women in Michigan — made possible by investing the money of her trade wisely in land and real estate.

Her scent of jasmine and frankincense quickly filled the interior of the truck's cab, quieting the smell of road dust and motor oil, and at the same time prompted Randy to grip the steering wheel self-consciously as his manhood stirred and reared boldly. She was undoubtedly the most beautiful creature he had ever seen, and he could not help but marvel at the sensual way she kept her full lips moist and glistening with the very tip of her suggestive tongue. She had deep set, dark, flashing eyes with a slender face that was framed with silky black, waist-length hair. And try as he may, he could not keep his eyes off of her perfectly molded, firm breasts, her tiny waist, or the way her hot-pink and black spandex suit revealed the most shapely legs that he'd ever seen.

Her sensuality was overwhelming, and for a moment, Randy forgot about Karen, and the real reason they had traveled so far to Detroit. All he could think of was the thumping mass in his groin and how he wanted to make love to this dark, lovely and mysterious creature, to touch her, and feel the strength of her thighs wrapped tightly around him.

Tanya seemed to sense his torment. She glanced quickly at his crotch, then attempted to break his preoccupation by asking, "How many times?" in a sharp, businesslike tone.

Randy, still hypnotized by her beauty, did not answer right away.

"How many?" she repeated, raising her voice slightly. "My stuff don't come cheap."

"F--five," Randy replied in a trembling voice. "Five," he repeated, conscious of the way Karen cut her eyes at him accusingly.

"Your girlfriend in on this, too?" Tanya asked as she looked at Karen suggestively.

"Y--yes." Karen stammered as she blushed deeply.

"That's cool," Tanya said with a nod as she motioned to Randy to start the truck. When the truck was moving, she pointed, and instructed him to drive in the direction of a row of wild pear trees growing in the distance.

As Randy slowly steered the pickup upon the grassy area and headed in the direction Tanya had pointed out to him — he was reminded of what his friends had said about Tanya's unique way of doing business.

It was said that Tanya always put herself "on the front line" in all of her business deals so that her lieutenants and colonels couldn't stab her in the back. And, by doing business in this unorthodox fashion — she had been able to secretly hold part-ownership in three-fourths of all the land located within the entire city of Detroit.

As they drew nearer, Randy noticed that there appeared to be a family picking pears from one of the trees. There was a man, a woman, and two children, all very shabbily dressed. The two children, a boy and a girl, were holding plastic, supermarket bags while the man and woman filled them with pears. *These must be the homeless people I keep reading about*, he said to himself.

As the pickup came to a stop, Randy subtly scanned the rear view mirror and found Karen's glaring eyes staring directly at him, pouting silently. *Not now, Karen*, he said to himself. *Please don't create a scene. Not in front of this made for loving woman.*

When Randy looked back out front, the young woman had stopped picking pears and was walking toward them. Tanya held up five manicured fingers — some sort of code, Randy supposed. At the signal, the young woman walked back to the pear tree, picked up a bag of pears, and returned to the truck. She handed the bag to Tanya. Moments later, the young woman was back at the tree gathering the ripening fruit with her family.

"Let's see your money," Tanya said as she held out her hand, palm up.

Randy quickly reached into his pocket nervously, withdrew a crisp, one-hundred dollar bill, and placed it on the smooth surface of Tanya's hand. She then handed him the bag of pears.

"For pears?" Randy asked, somewhat puzzled.

"For the pears, and what's in the bottom of the bag, honey."

Anxiously, Randy reached deep into the bottom of the bag, afraid that he was being ripped off. Underneath the smooth round fruit, he felt what he and Karen had driven all the way to Detroit for — five rocks of crack!

"Satisfied?" Tanya asked as she took the bill Randy had given her and folded it in half. Then, she folded it again. Next, she spread her legs ever so slightly to reveal a concealed velcro opening in the front of her spandex jumpsuit. Randy groaned audibly as he watched her insert the bill into the opening. In a flash, the bill was gone — swallowed by the crevice just like an automated teller machine. He was still staring wide-mouthed at the inviting shadows of Tanya's legs, when suddenly, Karen slammed her elbow into his ribs.

Tanya exited the pickup truck, walked a few feet away, then turned and blew them a kiss followed by a wave of good-bye.

When the exotic creature had gone, Randy and Karen cranked up their pickup and headed back for rural Michigan. As they entered the freeway, they noticed workmen putting up yet another billboard. Only this time, the advertisement read — THE PISTONS WIN . . . AGAIN.

Mission . . . accomplished.

* * *

The Awakening of Hanna Lee

by
Herbert R. Metoyer, Jr.

For Hanna Lee, days had no beginnings, and the nights, no ends. Everything was the same, chained together end to end with not one visible link, at least, none that she could readily identify. Everything the same. One piece. One piece of space. One piece of time, stretching out to eternity like an endless railroad track that came from nowhere in one direction and went to the same place in the other.

It hadn't always been that way. There was a time in the past when things were a lot different; a time when she had a better grip on life and a little something more to say about what she did and how she wanted to do it. That ended with Big Lou. He changed all that — brought her down and stomped her face right into the fucking ground. Sweet talking, Big Louis Bordeaux standing on the outside of the church during a gospel sing dressed in a powder blue, double breasted suit, his curly hair slicked down with half-a-can of Tuxedo hair grease, and looking to all the world like he was just another displaced white boy from cross the tracks.

She had come to Beaux Bridge, Louisiana from Mississippi in 1930, in the back of a back-country bus filled with exhaust fumes, sweating bodies, stale perfume, and a lunch bag filled with funky, day-old chicken to look after her sick aunt. She was twenty-six-years old at the time, still unmarried — still searching for Mr. Right.

In Mississippi, fair-skinned, colored men with *good hair* were rare. It was different in Louisiana.

Here, they were quite common, speaking their peculiar type of English with a Creole accent that she found to be just as captivating as it was frustrating.

All her life, she had dreamed of having such a man — a good looking one with a decent grade of hair. She could blame her mother for that. *"Hanna, don't be bringing none of them nappy-head boys around here talking about getting married. Think about your children first, and for God's sake, do try to find somebody who can improve your stock,"* she used to say almost daily. She didn't totally disagree with her mother, so in reality, she supposed it wasn't all her mother's fault. It was common knowledge that the fair-skinned negroes usually got the better jobs and were spoken of more kindly by the whites. That had certain advantages and she did not object to using them for her own benefit — well, not her own personal benefit, but more for that of her children. She was just a little too dark to fit in that — *hallowed category.*

Big Lou. What a sweet talking man he was — talked himself right into her house within two weeks after her Aunt Helena had died. Wouldn't hit a lick at a snake. Spent all of his time hanging around up on the block, talkin' shit and holding his dick, while she sweated over the board, ironing and lifting two and three pound chunks of hot, cast iron from buckets filled with smouldering coals.

Lou gambled a lot. When he won, she didn't see him for two — sometimes, three days. And when he lost, more often than not, he brought his whiskey-smelling friends home and sweet talked her into satisfying his debts with her body. At the time, it didn't seem to matter. Lou was five years younger than she was, and in her desperation to hold on to him, she would have done almost anything he asked. One thing she could say about Lou though — he never messed around on her, and he never once raised his voice in anger. She had to give him credit for that. *Sho'did.*

When the baby was born, Lou took one look at it, sat down, and cried like a baby. Three weeks later, when it was obvious to everyone that the baby was not his, he left — caught the Missouri-Pacific for Chicago. Left, while she was at work ironing white folk's clothes. Left, without one word of good-bye, just a hastily written note saying that he had borrowed the sixty dollars she had saved. A real low down, dirty, sweet-talking, bastard. She never heard from Lou again, not once in all the eight years that had gone by. What a fool she had been.

For a long time, she waited, hoping for his return. Sometimes, on especially lonely days, she used to get up and walk clear across town to the train depot just to watch it pull into the station. And when the conductors, dressed in their square, black caps, had unloaded and loaded their passengers, she would stand in the middle of the tracks watching in the distance long after they and their train had departed, cursing, and wondering how many fucking-fools it took to lay the many miles of hot, steel rails it took to run all the way up to Chicago.

But, she didn't do that anymore. She stopped once she realized how foolish she was being. Nowadays, she didn't even go near the station, and on the days when the wind carried the sound of their steam whistles to her side of town, she would press the palms of her hands to her ears to blot out their sickening wail. How she hated railroad trains — the way they screamed into the station wheezing and hollering, and blowing coal soot and smoke on everybody. She hated them too, for the effect they had on the little black boys who churned through the neighborhood, all in a line, their hands on each other's hips, playing choo choo train, and dreaming hopeless dreams of becoming conductors, firemen, and engineers when all the best of them could ever hope to be was nothing but a shit-eating, ass-kissing porter. But most of all, she hated them because they took people away to faraway places — like Chicago.

Wearily, she got up from her rumpled bed, her sheets red in spots from the blood of squashed mosquitoes, and smelling heavily of sweat and dried semen mingled with light traces of urine. This day just had to be different. Something had to happen today — something that would set the small, southern town of Beaux Bridge back on its heels and silence every single, bible-toting, gossiping tongue. Something that would be remembered for many years on down the road, and something that would prove to all that — a whore didn't have to stay a whore for the rest of her life.

With some effort, she walked over to her armoire, poked through her dresses until she found a deep-rose colored, clingy, satin chemise with white ribbons laced across the shoulders and across its low cut neckline. She had ordered it over a year ago from a Spiegel mail order book. The tags were still attached. She had ordered it just for this special occasion — the day that she would shine. The day she would change her life and start all over. No more whoring. No more sweaty, unwashed bodies straining between her legs and crushing her with their weight. No more squeezing into overcrowded bar rooms and juke joints, having to display her flesh and bare her breasts to be pawed at by any beastly creature with the desire to do so. No more taking their abuses, and no more dodging knives and broken beer bottles hurled across rooms in fits of anger. That was all in the past. Today was the start of something new — the day of her *awakening.*

She threw the dress across her bed, started a fire in her wood stove, and heated several large pots of water. When the water was hot, she poured it into the size-three metal wash tub that sat in the middle of her tiny kitchen. Then, she got a fresh wash cloth, a bar of lye soap, stepped into the tub, and bathed her body, paying particular attention to full, shapely breasts, her pride and joy, and sometimes — the cause of much of her sadness. For even though she felt that she had much more to offer a good man other than an appealing figure with ample buttocks and strong thighs, no one appeared to be at all interested. No one. There was not one person who gave a good Goddamn, or cared about what she thought, or how she felt, or nothing. All they seemed to care about was her ass and tits — *ass and tits.*

When her bath was finished, Hanna dried her body, then went to her dresser and prepared her face, being careful to avoid the use of too much makeup. What emerged in the mirror after all her efforts was a pleasant looking woman with a honey-brown complexion. It was not an especially beautiful face, but it was one that possessed a certain amount of character, reinforced by a full mouth that turned up slightly at the corners. No, she was not a young woman, but a woman of thirty-six hard, lonely, and frustrating years. Although she had looked at the face in the mirror many times in the past, today was the first time she happened to notice that there was a new light shining brightly in her tired eyes — one that confirmed and erased any previous doubts that she had had about her decision. And knowing that, she was suddenly filled with a deep sense of relief.

Her toilette completed, she searched through her dresser until she found a halfway decent pair of drawers. She pulled these on with meticulous care, pulling them high and prancing in place until they fitted snugly about her wide hips. Then, she reached beneath her bed, retrieved a pair of stockings she had worn the previous night, and rolled them up the calves of her muscular legs, securing them there with two fancy, black and red garters. Next, she slipped into her new, mail order dress and stepped into a pair of white, high heeled, sling pumps. With that done, she checked herself again in the mirror, and smiled.

Satisfied that she looked especially presentable, she slung her purse over her shoulder and went into her eight-year-old daughter's room.

"Collette," she whispered softly as she shook the dark skinned child awake. "Collette, wake up darling."

"Yes, maman?"

"Look, honey, your maman is going out for awhile — to get her hair pressed. When you get up, there are some sandwiches for you in the ice box. Be sure to brush your teeth and comb your hair. And, if I'm not back by sun down, take this note . . . " she stopped, dug into her purse, and found a neatly folded piece of paper. "Take this note over to your school teacher's house, give it to her, and ask Mrs. Miller to let you stay there until I get back. Okay?"

"Yes, maman."

"And don't forget your teeth and hair," she reminded her daughter as she put on her white, wide brimmed, Sunday straw hat and walked out the door into the bright light of an already sweltering sun. *I really must do something about my roses*, she said to herself as she observed the heavy growth of bitter weeds that seemed to be threatening to overrun her small front yard.

"Good morning, Mrs. Pearl," she yelled to her cranky, old neighbor who stood in her front yard leaning on her walking cane and glaring in her direction. "Nice, hot, sunshiny day, ain't it?"

The old, woman nodded coldly, then turned and hobbled quickly away toward the side of her small, unpainted, shotgun house.

"Mrs. Pearl," she yelled, "you got that old goose locked up in 'is pen?"

The old lady pretended not to hear and continued on around her house.

"I mean it, Mrs. Pearl," she yelled louder. "I got me a stick, and if that goose come out here messin' with me I'm gon' beat every feather he got off his butt!"

With no reply, Hanna shrugged her shoulders, walked out to her gate, and peered cautiously up and down the street in both directions. It was just too damn hot to be running from nobody's goose this early in the morning — the meanest, neck-stretching, wing-flapping goose in four states — needed to be in somebody's cooking pot instead of out here pestering decent folks. How she hated *gooses* and railroad trains.

Satisfied that the coast was clear, she headed quickly down the street toward May Belle's beauty shop thinking about her sweet, precocious, little daughter and how different life would be for her once she got things in order. Mrs. Miller had said that Collette was one of her brightest students; that she could go far with the right kind of help. Well today, she was going to do her best to make sure of that. *Sho'was.*

As she rounded the corner, she almost bumped headlong into James Tee who was sweeping the steps that led into his tiny corner store.

"Hold on, gal. Bad luck to step on a man's broom like that."

"Ain't no more bad luck for me, James Tee. Nothing but good stuff from now on."

"Well, I'm sho'nuff glad you think so. Me, if I didn't have me no bad luck, I'd really be in po' shape. Gal, you sho' looking fine this day. What you doing out so early?"

"Why, thank you, James Tee. I'm looking fine, 'cause I feel fine. Haven't felt this fine in a long time. Just couldn't lay in that funky, old bed a minute longer."

"Well, I can see that. Don't nobody in the world fill out a dress like you do. Lord, you something else. You gon' be busy about 12:30?"

"Yes, I am, James Tee. I certainly am."

"That's too bad. I was gonna suggest that I drop by and see you 'bout then. I ain't got the money right now, but you know I'm good for it. I'll have plenty Friday when the mill pay off. Half the people in the Quarters owe me."

"Thanks, but not today, James Tee. Me — I got some other fish to fry. Besides, I got to meet the 12:45 today."

"What you doing, taking a trip somewhere?"

"Maybe. Maybe not."

"Well, while you're deciding, come on in out the sun and have a cold sodawater on me."

Hanna looked at her watch, decided she still had plenty of time, so she said, "Okay. Don't mind if I do."

James Tee dropped his broom and pulled the Holsom Bread screen door open for her eagerly. She had hardly stepped across the threshold into the dimly lit store before she felt him crowd in behind her and brush the flats of his hands over her taunt buttocks.

"Cut it out, James. No sense getting yourself worked up. I told you — ain't nothing shaking today."

"Just fooling around, Hanna Lee. Well, what's your flavor? I got Nehi Orange, RC Cola, Nu-Grape, and some of coldest Delaware Punch south of the North Pole."

"I'll take a Nu-Grape, if you don't mind," she replied as she sat down on a low stool and crossed her legs somewhat carelessly. She saw the look of lust that quickly clouded James' eyes, but since he was treating her to a cold drink, she decided not to bother adjusting her short skirt. She had made it a practice long ago — to never take a nickel from a man without giving something of equal value in return. The Nu-Grape wasn't worth much, but it was worth something, she supposed.

"Well, what about tonight, Hanna? I'll be closing up here about nine."

"Baby, I can't promise nothing about tonight. I told you, I got plans. And if everything goes well, you just might have to start taking your business over to Willie Mae's."

"Willie Mae? Hanna, you know I don't mess around with no Willie Mae. There ain't a woman north of New Orleans who can do it like you do. And that's the God's truth. I rather go out there and climb me one of Little Red's billy goats than to crawl up on Willie Mae's bony, little butt."

"I know what you mean," Hanna laughed, "but I can't help you today, baby. James, you think I could have a piece of one them pig foots?"

"You know you can, Hanna," James Tee replied as he stepped around the counter and spun off the top of a large jug that rested between a jar of stage plank cakes and another filled with bright colored, candy jaw breakers. With a concerned smile, he stuck a

37

slightly rusty fork into the large jug smelling heavily of vinegar and pulled out one of the smallest he could find.

Hanna took the dripping-juice pig foot, thanked James, then leaned over and bit deeply into the soft bones with the edges of her perfectly spaced teeth.

"Hanna, I swear I sho'nuff do be hurting. You got them hot legs of yours messin' with my mind. Gal, I'm hard as a granite rock and twice as solid. Lawdy, look at what I got me here," he pleaded, squeezing his crotch tightly.

"Shit, James Tee I done seen your stuff before. Now, quit trying to mess with me. It's too damn hot to be getting my nerves upset behind your bullshit. I ain't the only 'hoe in this raggedy-assed town. Now, find somebody else. Me — I got to be going 'cause if I hang around here arguing with you, you gon' make me miss the train."

"Ain't trying to get you mad, Hanna. But, you know I'm good for the money."

"I know you are, James. You done hoped me out heaps of times, and I thanks you for that. But, this ain't about no money, baby. It ain't about nothing like that. It's about something completely unrelated — something, you don't know nothing about. And thanks again for the snack," Hanna added as she lifted her body from the stool, "It ain't good to eat and run, but I just got to see if May Belle can do my hair."

* * *

"Hanna," May Belle said delightfully as Hanna opened the door and jingled a small goat's bell. "Girl, what you doing out and about so early — and all dressed up, too. Ain't she looking good, Shirley?"

"Just like new money," Shirley replied, looking up

at Hanna undereyed while May Belle prepared to pass a smoking, hot comb through her short, rough hair.

"You just stopping to chat or do you want your hair done?"

"I want my hair done, May Belle, but I don't have a whole lot of time. I want to try and catch the 12:45."

"I wouldn't worry. Most the time that train's a half-hour late, anyway. I swear, there ain't one engineer on the Missouri-Pacific line who can tell you the time of day. And that's the God's truth."

Hanna laughed. "I hope you right. I lost a lot of time down the street there talking to James Tee."

"Bet that old coon was begging for pussy, wasn't he?"

"You know you right."

"That James Tee is something else. Begs everybody — one hard-up old coon. Last week, some of the kids caught him parked out behind the school house with — guess who?"

"Willie Mae?"

"No, child," May Belle doubled over with laughter. "He was out there with Lena's fat ass spread out in the back end of his picking-up truck — her and all her three hundred pounds."

Everyone laughed heartily. Suddenly, Shirley yelled. "Watch it, May Belle. Shit, you burning up my damn ear."

"Sorry, Shirley," May Belle said with another chuckle. "It just cracks me up every time I think about Lena in the back end of that raggedy truck. You know, I don't know why Rose put up with James Tee carrying the way like he do. I know she knows what's happening. He provides for her well enough though, so I guess she just satisfied with that. But, if it was me, and he was my husband, I'd be done beat the shit outta him a long time ago. A man like that, just ain't no good for a decent woman."

"Ain't it the truth."

A short while later, Shirley left, and Hanna took her place in the burning chair. "May Belle," she said solemnly. "You have fixed my hair at least a thousand times, and you have always fixed it just fine. But today, I want you to do me a favor and make me more beautiful than you have ever done before. Make me look like a real lady — like a Sunday school teacher would do just fine."

"I'll try, Hanna. I'll do the very best I can. Now relax, and let old May Belle work her magic. When I finish, every man in town will be sniffing behind you like pack of broke-dick dogs."

Hanna closed her eyes and breathed deeply of the aroma of jasmine and honeysuckles mixed with that of roasting hair and Dixie Peach pomade, an odor that she found neither delightful nor offensive. Just another necessary odor like any other necessary odor, like the smell of saw dust from the mill on an easterly wind, or the smell of burning coal deep inside the bowels of a belching locomotive — common everyday odors that you either had to ignore, or just learn to live with.

Big, bad, good-looking Lou Bordeaux,
   Lord, where did he go?
Left his big-leg whore with a baby,
   caught the train to Chica-go.

Hanna smiled to herself at her clever little rhyme, then made a mental note to write it down before she forgot. How she hated railroad trains . . . .

"Wake up, Hanna. I done duded you up like never before. Take a look in the mirror and tell me what you think?"

Hanna raised up sleepily and looked expectantly into the dimly lit mirror. She was pleased. "It's a good job, May Belle. Ain't nobody else in the world who can set hair like you do. Nobody. And that's the God's truth."

"Well, that's a nice compliment, Hanna. I do try."

"Ain't it the truth," Hanna said as she reached into her purse and handed May Belle three, one dollar bills.

"Hanna, I don't mean to pry. But tell me — are you expecting Lou to be on that train?"

"That low down, dirty bastard? Not on your life. If I even thought Lou was on that train, I'd be out there now pulling up cross-ties with my bare hands — trying to find some way to make that fucker derail."

"And I'd be out there trying to help you, too." May Belle laughed at the thought. "Anyway, Hanna, you and me been friends for a long time, and all I want is what's best for you. You don't have to tell me your business, I don't want to know. But, just in case you might be leaving, please don't forget me, and write when you can."

"Nothing like that, May Belle. In fact, don't be a bit surprised if you happen to find me sittin' up in Grace Baptist Church tomorrow evening or the day after."

"Go on, gal. Get outta here before you miss that train."

Hanna, got up and embraced May Belle fondly. They held on to each other for a long moment, quietly, each just a little reluctant to let the other go. Almost unnoticeably, May Belle's warm, soft hands wandered up the sides of Hanna's back and came to rest gently against her flushed cheeks. In the next moment, they were kissing, full mouthed, hungrily, and passionately.

"I'm so sorry, Hanna," May Belle said as she

suddenly stepped back, somewhat embarrassed. "I don't know what overcame me — something I've wanted to do for a long time. It just seemed like something come and told me — do it today."

"Don't apologize, May Belle. It ain't about nothing."

"You sure?"

"Yes. I'm sure."

"Hanna?"

"Yes."

"Can I — again? Just once before you go?"

"Yes," Hanna replied as she melted into May Belle's hot, sticky arms. "The train . . . don't forget the . . . ."

* * *

It was almost 12:15 by the time Hanna arrived at the depot station and stepped upon the hot, concrete ramp that stretched between the depot and the edge of the tracks. The heat was unbearable, and she was sweating like a horse from her exertions. As she paused to blot the moisture from her face and the visible parts of her full breasts with a tiny, white, handkerchief, the ticket agent came out the "White Only" door studying the face of a worn, golden, pocket watch.

"Excuse me, sir," she asked politely, "is the train on time today?"

The agent inserted the watch back into the top pocket of his vest, looked up at her somewhat annoyed, then said, "Won't be more than five minutes late, today."

While the ticket agent was squinting down the long lengths of hot steel, a playful breeze blew up the ramp and tugged at the hem of her soft, clinging, satin skirt. She closed her knees quickly and pressed it back down with the flat of one hand while reaching with the other to steady her white, wide brimmed hat — but, not before the agent caught a fleeting glimpse of her shapely legs. He smiled.

"You getting on board today?"

"I don't know for sure, sir."

"Well, if you're going, better make up your mind. Train don't wait for nobody."

"I know, sir," she said as she watched him turn and re-enter the "White Only" door, swinging it wide.

At that moment, a baby inside squalled. A little nosey, Hanna quickly glanced over the agent's shoulder and observed several white passengers sitting comfortably beneath huge, rotating fans talking, eating fruit, and reading crumpled up newspapers. The door slammed shut with a bang, causing Hanna to flinch. A little embarrassed, she lifted her nose haughtily, adjusted her shoulder bag, and walked sassily away, passing the outside "Colored Only" ticket window to the end of the ramp where she stepped off into a long bed of gray, marble colored, cinder rocks. Once she got her footing, she continued to the colored waiting area which was nothing more than a row of weather-beaten benches beneath the baggage loading area overhang just in front of the place where the white folks tied up their mangy horses and mules. Two old, black men sat on one of the benches with their legs crossed, fanning flimsy, funeral-home fans, and conversing quietly. Further down, several younger, black men with severely worn, porter's caps sat on small, narrow wagons filled with white folk's luggage, dozing, and waiting listlessly for the 12:45.

"Is that you, Hanna?" one of the old men asked.

"Yes, Mr. Clem. It's me."

"You going off somewhere today?"

"No, I doubt it. Wouldn't mind to. But never had enough money to catch me a ticket. No, I just thought I'd come down and watch it pull in."

"Well, you picked a good day. They got them a new train. Fastest thing on iron wheels — must have ten driving. Don't take more'n hour to get from here to New Orleans."

"You don't say."

"Yeah, they took old, number Eight-Eleven off last week. Got her switching in the switch yard now."

"That was a good, old engine — number Eight-Eleven was," Jimbo, the other old man added.

"Yeah, she was. But, I tell you, white folks is something else. They ain't never satisfied, not from one day to the next. Always hauling up something new."

"Ain't it the truth," Hanna added solemnly as she crossed her arms and reared back on one leg.

Suddenly, a steam whistle sounded in the distance. Hanna raised her head and squinted down the long, double line of heat distorted tracks. She could see it coming, puffing like an angry dragon and discoloring the whole horizon with filthy black smoke.

Slowly, the depot came to life. The porters slid off the wagons, adjusted their caps, and put on their *Uncle Tom's* faces. The white folks gathered their children, hand baggage, and lunches, and filed out of their "White Only" door. The old, black men nudged one another and sat up in their seats perkily, their eyes filled with childlike excitement.

"Clem, when that train stops — how far down the track do the colored cars be at?"

"Ain't no telling, Hanna. Most of the time you can get on down there by that silver, flag pole. Sometimes, it be way on down pass that. Jes' depends on how far the engineer feels like making the colored folks walk. Ain't no telling."

"Thank you, Mr. Clem," she said as she started off down the side of the track, stepping high in the large cinder rocks and experiencing some difficulty due to the height of her heels. *Yes, very definitely. Today was the day*, she said to herself with some excitement. *Sho'was.*

The steam whistle blew again. She stopped and looked up. It was getting close, and at intervals, she could hear the engineer applying the brakes gently, slowing Big Bertha on down.

The breeze out on the open rails was stronger, so she lowered her head into the hot, creosote smelling wind, held on to her hat, and started walking again. She was well pass the silver, signal pole when she looked up again. It was much closer now, so close that she could make out the details of the low-riding cow catcher quite clearly despite the hindrance of the long, shimmering waves of heat.

Without a second thought, she stepped upon the slope of the track bed, almost falling in the process, and made her way shakily to the center of the tracks, still holding tightly to the top of her white, wide brimmed hat with one hand and clutching the thin strap of her shoulder bag with the other. When she had steadied the feet below her quivering legs on a severely cracked cross-tie, she looked up — directly into the oily face of the engineer who leaned out of the cab, his eyes wide with alarm, his arms waving and tugging frantically for relief valves and shiny, metal handles. Wheels squealed miserably amidst mile long showers of sparks, while steam whistles blew out their guts, loudly and painfully. And all she could think of to do at the time was — smile. God, how she hated a fucking railroad train . . . .

Images

**by
Barbara Hunter**

> *Have you chosen to close the curtains*
> *On the windows*
> *of life,*
> *So you won't be able to see*
> *Your reflection in the glass?*
> *Then*
> *Come with me*
> *Part the curtains*
> *Ever so slightly*
> *Your reflection will not appear*
> *Only the images*
> *of your mind*
> *Will dance*
> *Before your eyes —*

She was a laser light show in a room of bellicose darkness — effervescent, commanding, demanding attention by her mere presence — mature for someone so young, self- assured, expectant, and hopeful — well fed and bred, yet, not with the arrogance one would expect — attractive but not gaudy with a lock of hair that kept falling into her face. "Here for the summer . . ." she said, ". . . from New York."

"Watch out for the wolves," I cautioned her during our introduction, smiling the coded smile we women of all ages transmit knowingly to one another.

Bree had just arrived in Detroit, visiting relatives and working as a laboratory technician for the summer to finance another trip.

The average age of the work force was forty — a

group of hardened individuals, paranoid and cynical about life. In a short time, Bree's arrival brought a complete metamorphism to this odd and sometimes hostile group. Flowers of courtesy, politeness, consideration, and humaneness began to grow in a place that was once a barren ground of indifference.

Her unique approach to the seen and unseen obstacles of life bewildered us all. "Wonderful challenges," she would say to no one in particular while bouncing around in her *Ree-boks* — those famous shoes so highly regarded by all youngsters as all occasion footwear.

In doing so, she generated a considerable amount of envy among the rest of us who viewed her youthful inexperience and enthusiasm with a suspicious eye. This went on all summer long. I, however, was impressed with the young woman's glowing appreciation of life, and the way she went about taking care of business with her *Wonderful challenges* war cry.

"By the way," I inquired during the few remaining hours of her last day, "will you be returning next summer?"

"No, I'm going to spend next summer in Florida visiting my other son."

"Your other son? No shit — you're kidding! You look too young to have children." *Perhaps — he is being cared for by relatives*, I think to myself.

In an attempt to placate my curiosity, I asked, "How old are your little darlings?"

"Twenty-four and twenty-two," she said, but her voice was drowned by a sudden bombardment of loud voices and noise in the area.

"What?" I asked with a shout.

"Twenty-four and twenty-two!" she shouted back.

Filled with stark confusion, I non-intentionally

blurted out what I was thinking, "Well, how old are you?"

"Forty-eight, and loving every minute of it!" she responded loud enough for everyone to hear, grinning all the while as heads turned and mouths dropped. *Mine — dropped the lowest.*

* * *

A Father For Malik

by
Dianne White Morris

Tiny beads of perspiration surfaced on Malik Watson's caramel-colored face. It was much too warm for the pullover sweater that Momma had insisted he wear that morning. It was Friday, and now that school was out for the week-end, the sweater hung sheik-like on his head as he and his friend, Dejuan, jogged past small, square houses with neatly kept lawns.

"Hey, Malik, who's going to be your partner at the Father and Son Olympics next month?" asked Dejuan, his long legs moving as smoothly as his voice crooned.

"Don't know — yet, but I'll find somebody," Malik said breathlessly.

"Yeah, sure you will," Dejuan said, darting his eyes at his friend. "I hope you know mother can't be your partner," he said slyly.

"Yeah, I know," said Malik. *Don't let me be the only sixth grader without a partner again this year*, he thought. "Come on, I'll race you to Mr. Chaney's yard."

Off they went. Malik could see Mr. Chaney shifting to and fro in the green glider on his front porch eating his favorite — roasted peanuts.

The boys arrived at the old man's gate completely out of breath. Smoots, Mr. Chaney's collie, stood slowly, stretched, and let out three loud barks, warning him of the intruders.

Mr. Chaney rubbed his large belly. "Hello boys," he said, popping a few nuts into his mouth.

"Hi-ya Mr. Cee," said Malik. He smiled, showing

his small even teeth. His lips then made kissing sounds as he coaxed Smoots off of the porch and away from Mr. Chaney's side. "Good boy," he cooed as he smoothed the old dog's coat. "How old is Smoots, Mr. Chaney?"

Mr. Chaney chuckled. "Sixteen-years-old. That's one- hundred and twelve in man's years. Been a mighty good companion, too, with the missus gone on to Heaven and all." He took a deep breath and let it out just as hard.

Malik knew when someone was sad, and Mr. Chaney could sure use some cheering up. "How about I come over and play you some checkers tomorrow Mr. Cee? I've got some chores to do, but afterward, I could—you know—keep you company."

"Sure," said Mr. Chaney, "and why don't you ask your momma if you can go to church with me Sunday morning. I know you'll like it."

"I'll ask. But, I'm sure she won't mind though," said Malik while scratching his knee.

Mr. Chaney began to rock again, and the boys could hear the squeak of the glider as they strolled away slowly down the street.

Dejuan wrinkled his face and pinched his nose. "Do you know we have only two days before we have to go back to school, and you're going to spend them on an old man and his snaggle-toothed mutt? I know life can be boring when you don't have a father around, but be serious! My dad's taking me to the game tomorrow, and Sunday, we're going to Crystal Lake . . ."

"Dejuan," Malik interrupted, "if you're going to start bragging again, I'd just as soon walk home alone. Anyway, you act as if my daddy ran away or something. He died, Dejuan. Died! How can you be so dumb sometimes?" Malik shouted angrily.

"Go on home by yourself. See if I care," Dejuan yelled as he gave Malik a quick shove that sent him tumbling to the ground. "And that'll teach you to call me dumb!" he added before darting off.

Malik got up and yanked the sweater from his head angrily. He saw a yellowish caterpillar inching across the sidewalk. "That Dejuan makes me so mad . . . ." he yelled as he raised his foot high into the air and poised to squash the furry worm as it squirmed slowly toward its destination. "Don't worry," he said aloud as he lowered his foot, "I'm not going to hurt you. Wanna know something? You're going to be a pretty nice butterfly one of these days."

When the caterpillar had moved off into the grass, Malik sighed and started for home.

On the following Saturday, the morning sun peeked over the horizon into Malik's neighborhood and revealed the stocky figure of the boy raking leaves from his front yard.

"Whew!" Malik said, casting the rake to the ground. He bounded into the house, slamming the wooden door behind him with a bang.

"What are you doing out so early, Malik?" his mother called from her bedroom. "You know I don't like you out the house while I'm still asleep."

Malik didn't rightfully know just why he had awakened before the crack of dawn. "Sorry, momma," he said, after a moment. "I guess I wanted to get done early so that I could visit Mr. Chaney today. Did you forget?"

"No, I didn't forget," his mother, Mrs. Watson, replied as she wrapped a robe around her shoulders and padded into the living room. "Mr. Chaney called while you were working. He had to take Smoots to the veterinarian this morning. I . . ."

"Smoots? Oh, no! Mr. Chaney told me that Smoots was a hundred and twelve. He's too old to get sick." Suddenly, Malik's head reeled. "I feel kind of wobbly inside," he added, holding his stomach with one hand and his head with the other. "Momma, why is there death?"

"Malik, nothing on this earth lives forever. Life is a cycle. Take the flowers — they grow tall and beautiful in the summer, but when winter comes, they die. Don't they?"

"Yes."

"It's the same with animals and people. Most of us live to an ripe old age. But, accidents can happen — like when your daddy died. It's really nobody's fault. It just happens, that's all." Mrs. Watson hugged her son and rubbed his wooly-soft hair. "You miss daddy, don't you?"

"Yes," Malik nodded. "It makes me feel sad at times. Like yesterday, Dejuan was teasing me because I don't have anyone to enter the Olympics with again this year."

Mrs. Watson shook her head. "People do say things to hurt your feelings, and usually, when they do, they themselves are the ones hurting inside. Want to know something? I miss your daddy an awful lot myself. But, that doesn't mean we give up on living. You and I are going on. Together, we will make it — just you wait and see."

"I'm glad we're together, momma," Malik whispered seriously. "And when I get grown, I'm gonna take care of you."

The phone rang and Malik scurried to answer it.

"Hello. Hello?" He said. He listened attentively for several moments, then hung up. "Smoots is alright, Momma. He sneaked into Mr. Cee's peanut barrel and got a terrible bellyache. The doctor told Mr. Cee

— no more peanuts for Smoots. From now on, he can only have beef bones for his snacks!"

Malik laughed, and so did his mother. Moments later, he was scurrying out the door, off to play checkers with Mr. Cee.

* * *

When Mr. Chaney stepped up on Malik's porch the next morning, Malik was waiting, fully dressed with his blue slacks creased, white shirt crisp, and his shoes shining like new money, gazing at himself in the mirror. Just saying the word church tasted good in his mouth, and he was excited about it. Maybe, he'd see some of his classmates there. He hoped so. "I'm ready, Mr. Cee!" he shouted.

"My, my, don't you look fine. Yes siree, mighty sporty," said Mr. Chaney. "I was just telling your momma, I've got a surprise for you."

"What is it?" Malik asked eagerly. Mr. Chaney and Momma just smiled.

"Wait until after Sunday school, Malik." Momma said, waving as Malik walked to the car with Mr. Chaney.

When Malik settled into the seat of Mr. Chaney's old Ford, he felt as if he was riding on a cloud. They rode past familiar sights until they reached a simple, white building. Many people were walking into the wide, double doors. Mr. Chaney parked his car, they got out, and as they followed the line quietly inside, Mr. Chaney placed an arm around Malik's shoulders.

Sunlight filtered in through brightly colored windows and he heard soft music twirling over head.

Directed to his seat, he sat beside Roger Fielding, a boy from his school. Miss Rochelle, the Sunday school teacher, passed the lesson books around.

"Today," she said, "we're going to learn about God. Can anyone tell me why he is called our Heavenly Father?"

Roger raised his hand. "Because, He loves us so much!" he said quickly.

Malik raised his dark eyebrows until they almost reached his even darker hairline. A smile larger than any other shined on his face.

When Sunday school was over, a hush came over the entire church. Suddenly, applause thundered in his ears. Malik glanced around, stretching his neck to see a huge man standing in the back of the church.

The pastor made the announcement. It was Deke Jamison, former coach of the Angel's football team. Deke had come back home.

Deke lumbered to the front of the congregation and stood silent. Then, he spoke in a deep voice. "I'm very glad," he said, "to be in the house of the Lord, once more, and to be a follower of Christ . . . ." *Hey, Deke Jamison is a Christian!* thought Malik. ". . . I'm also thankful," Deke continued, "for people like Mr. Chaney who kept in touch with me while I was away. Come on up, Mr. Chaney."

Mr. Chaney blushed and rubbed his belly. He pushed himself from his seat and made his way to the front and stood next to Deke.

Malik stared in awe as the two men hugged. There was a tear in Deke's eye. Suddenly, Mr. Chaney looked in his direction and beckoned for him to join them.

Malik got up shakily and walked to the front, concentrating on his feet as he felt the eyes of everyone on him. After his long journey up the aisle, Malik shook Deke's hand, and while he was doing so,

Mr. Chaney bent low and whispered in his ear — *This is the surprise. Deke here, is going to be your partner in the father and son Olympics!*

Malik was so overcome with joy that he leaped up and down. Then, the three of them, him, Deke, and Mr. Chaney headed for the door. As they neared the rear of the church, Malik glanced up at a picture of Jesus, and suddenly he knew — the smile he saw on Jesus' face was meant especially for him.

* * *

Melody Unchained

**by
Suma**

It was one of those late-spring, almost summer days, when it seemed that everybody in thé universe was barbecuing or suntanning in their back yard or both. It was the kind of day when free spirits rejoiced.

Looking out of the tiny, barred window above my head, I encountered a brilliant patch of azure sky. A few tiny rays of sunlight entered my room and ensconced themselves on the sick-looking, pale green wall, hanging on as if for dear life. I imagined the rays ever deepening and crossing the tiled floor, as they would later in the day. From the current position of the rays, I figured it to be about eleven a.m. About the time, I surmised, that the kids would be attending their Saturday morning piano lessons.

Suddenly, I shuddered physically from an unexpected wave of depression. *Think present. Think future,* I told myself determinedly. *You've got Tracy and Lisa to think about. You have got to keep it together, so you can get out and help prepare them so they won't end up spending time in places like this.*

Whenever my thoughts fell upon the kids, my eyes usually welled with tears. My girls were still so young, so vulnerable. Their lives had always been permeated with the sordid reality of spouse abuse, the concomitant deprivation, and the intense hatred that finally, after seven years of hell, led to my stabbing Rick to death with a butcher knife in our kitchen. Oddly enough, considering the consequences, all I could think about at the time was whether the blood would stain the linoleum floor.

Of course, such an uncertain situation and the resulting maternal deprivation had to have had a profound effect on my daughters. And, although my mother was granted custody throughout the length of my incarceration in this hospital for the criminally insane, having a grandmother with them was just not enough. Tracy and Lisa needed me, and I — definitely — needed them. I smiled to myself, thinking of my girls, their fortitude, and the emotional stamina they displayed throughout the ordeal.

I looked forward to the weekly letters from home, filled with tasty tidbits. And the bimonthly Saturday afternoon phone calls to me from Tracy were ever so precious. They were all the more dear to me because I could only receive calls, I could not transmit out — hospital rules. Just one of many that I was subjected to.

"Melody Garrett, phone call!" The voice of Denise Willis cut through the fetid air. Denise was the most empathetic of all the attendants on my unit, going out of her way to treat us with dignity and respect. Being doubly oppressed (African-American and female), she well knew the effects of racism and sexism on Third World women. And on this all-female unit, the consequences of oppression were, for the most part, the very reasons for our incarceration.

With twinkling eyes and a flash of ivory, Denise appeared at the entrance to my room. "Come on, Melody," she said with urgency, "get a move on, girl. Tracy's on the horn."

"Thanks, Neecie," I said, smiling as I got up from the chair where I had been sitting and gazing at the meager sunlight that filtered in through my tiny window. "I was just wondering when I'm getting out of here, and what it'll be like for me once I'm out there. I look forward to leaving, but I'm scared, too — you know."

"I know that's right. Don't worry, baby. You'll make it. You're a survivor. I've seen many women come and go, but you've got the savvy to make it out there with your girls. Speaking of which, you better get to that phone fast before someone hangs it up." Another toothy grin, and Denise was gone.

I hurried to the phone, the only one available for patient use on the unit. "Hi, honey. How did your lessons go today?"

"Oh, fine, Mom. I'm starting to learn jazz piano, now. I really like it. Lisa's learning it, too. Mr. Jackson says jazz is original African-American music."

"Mr. Jackson is right. You keep at it, you hear me? And study hard, so you can make your mother proud. I can't stress that enough. Do what you have to do to excel, and don't take no mess from anybody, you hear? . . . Tracy, I have been here so long, and I miss you both so terribly. But, guess what? Dr. Rodriguez is talking about letting me out soon. Isn't that great?"

"Oh, Mom," my twelve-year-old said with excitement. Then, she began to cry.

I found this surprising. Tracy rarely showed her emotions. Unlike her ten-year-old sister, Lisa, who cried copiously at Rick's funeral, Tracy did not. Most of the time, she stared straight ahead, unmoved, like death was nothing more than another stage in the cycle of life. But six long years without a mother, along with impending adolescence and its accompanying hormonal changes, seemed to be bringing about some emotional changes about that Tracy was finding difficult to understand and explain . . . .

"Mom," Tracy continued. "I miss you so much. So

does Lisa, and Grandma, too. Are you really going back to school?"

"Yes, honey," I answered. "I'm going back to major in psychology — maybe work in a shelter for battered women. I should definitely qualify with my experiences with your dad, his threats, and mental and physical abuse towards us. You know, Tracy, I only want the best for you girls. I want you to grow up strong, intelligent African-American women. Like I always say . . ."

"Knowledge is power," we both spoke with one voice. Tracy laughed and it was good to hear her laugh again.

"You know, Mom," Tracy continued, suddenly adopting a serious tone, "I miss you, and I don't think you were wrong. Daddy was abusive to us all. You couldn't take anymore, and you snapped. I just wish it could have been handled some other way."

"And me, too. But at the time, baby, he didn't leave me a choice. You know that. Every time I'd leave, he'd find me. Then it would be worse than before. I hate what I did, but looking back, maybe it was best in the long run. I need all of you, now — more than ever before. With my discharge in sight, we'll be together again . . . ." My eyes welled with tears, and for a moment, I could not speak for the lump in my throat. "This time, Tracy honey, things will be better. You'll see. We'll . . ."

"Garrett." The icy voice of Mrs. Borden cut off the rest of my thoughts and left them unsaid. "Get off the phone. After you leave here," she added caustically, "you can talk all you want. You haven't been discharged yet."

"All right, Mrs. Borden," I said, staring straight ahead so that I could avoid the head nurse's menacing glare. "Take care, Tracy," I said softly. "I love you."

"I love you, too. Bye, Mom."

The phone clicked. I hung up quickly, but not quickly enough to appease Mrs. Borden.

"You know the rules, Garrett," she shouted as I retreated to my room. "Next time you overstep your bounds, you'll really hear from me!"

There was a time when I would have cursed her out, and simply continued talking. Invariably, the goon squad would have been called, and I would have been put in restraints and thrown into seclusion. This happened to me many, many times during the first two years after my arrival. But gradually, I learned to resist my initial impulse to rebel. And in most cases, I merely acknowledged her request and got off the phone quickly, lest I incur her wrath.

The whole process was a severe struggle on my part, and my struggling did not desist until I suddenly realized that obedience to hospital rules expedited one's release. It was a bitter pill to swallow, but it was finally paying off. The unit psychiatrist, Dr. Rodriguez, a Puerto Rican, who had seen me at my worst times, and had stuck with me through it all, was indeed, hinting about releasing me soon. He said, however, that it was going to be up to me to become a self-sustaining, productive citizen, if I hoped to resume my life with my family.

My first step, which, admittedly, took a long time, was in changing my combative behavior. This task was far from simple, since, at the time, I regarded everyone as a potential foe — even those who went out of their way to offer me their assistance.

The second step, which was even harder, lay in convincing the staff that I was rehabilitated, and therefore, ready for discharge — and believe me, I was. Six years was a long time for anyone to be away from their loved ones.

The remainder of the day passed uneventfully. I went to dinner (the most palatable meal there), worked in the kitchen washing dishes for two combined units, received my free, state cancer cigarettes as a reward for good behavior and work skills, then played spades until I received my usual roundup of nighttime meds about eleven p.m.

* * *

The next day, a Sunday, we were awakened at six in the morning. After making my bed, I dressed and forced my way into the usual lineup for morning meds. As I stepped up to the medication nurse, Ms. Kaplan, I noticed that she was smiling at me — something she rarely did. "After you take your meds, Dr. Rodriguez wants to see you, Garrett."

He's here? I said to myself in shock. *It's 6:30 in the morning, on Sunday, yet.*

I had no time to ponder her words. I quickly swallowed my meds and hurried down the hall, curious to know why I was being summoned so early in the morning.

The psychiatrist, by this time, was standing by his office door waiting for me. I saw the look on his face and my initial apprehension changed to one of relief and bridled expectation. It was a special look, wreathed in a big, gentle smile that widened as I approached.

"Well, Melody," he said as he invited me in and took a seat at his desk, still smiling broadly, "you look very nice today. How are you feeling?"

"Fine, Doctor. Just fine."

"You think you're ready to leave?"

I stared at Dr. Rodriguez, afraid to answer and wondering if his question was a trick, or a sick joke. Doctors have been known to do that — ask trick questions, and I wasn't too sure how I should respond.

Realizing that I wasn't going to answer, he went on somewhat more seriously, "Melody, you have, in the eyes of society, committed a crime, and although we acknowledge that it was done in self-defense, it was still a crime, nevertheless. But, based on the great improvements you have made during your stay here, myself and the whole staff feel that you are ready to resume your life. Your mother agrees. I spoke to her recently, and she is willing to return custody of your girls to you. So — what do you think of all this?"

I shook my head as if I was trying to clear it. It was all too sudden. I had lived for this day for the past six years, but now, the immediate prospect of being released was frightening, and it made me more than a bit apprehensive. I sat speechless, then slowly something else brushed aside my fears — a giant dose of happiness and yes, relief. Tons of it.

My diverse emotions must have been visible, for Dr. Rodriguez suddenly smiled again and leaned forward in his chair. "Melody," he said, lowering his voice conspiratorially, "I also believe that you have the intellect and empathy to be a superb therapist. You were very helpful here, and your sincerity is without question.

"Although you have been through a great ordeal, you are coming out on top. You faced all the issues we had to deal with, and you dealt with them in an exemplary manner. In our opinion, you have the potential for success — especially with the type of support you have from your family." Then, he leaned back and continued, "Well, that's it in a nutshell. So now, how do you feel about it — any comments?"

I blinked and shook my head again. "When can I leave?" was all I could think to say.

"Today, if you like. We'll keep you on meds for awhile — maybe, even reduce your haloperidol a bit. You aren't having any more racing thoughts, are you?"

"No, Doctor. My depression is about gone, too. I don't think I can ever thank you enough for your kindness, and your patience. You really did help me through a tough spot."

"That's good to hear, Melody. My job was easy. You did all the work. It's a psychiatrist's duty to help people to help themselves. In your case, I think we both succeeded admirably . . . . Would you like for your mother to pick you up this morning?"

"Yes, I would," I said with a nervous smile. I was about to get up when the doctor chuckled and said warmly, "Use my phone. We don't want to disturb Mrs. Borden on a beautiful day like today — now, do we?"

"Muchas gracias!" I replied, as I took a deep breath and reached for the phone.

* * *

The Greenfields

by
R. K. Jones

No one told us. They just arrived one day — a day still wet from an early rain. We gathered quickly and stood somewhere between fascination and awe. Some of us began to cry. The rest fought back their tears with that unique childhood defiance that displayed neither hatred nor fear; each of us expressing and exciting sorrow bound up with feelings that we could not yet define.

In a trembling voice, and to no one in particular, Dennis Miller asked, "Why are they doing it?"

"They's white, ain't they?" said Lester Adams, a hard, ashy-black boy with hot, black eyes. "They can do anything they want to."

Their big, smoky machines tore through our Greenfields, pushed over our trees and raked them through our berry bushes. Endless iron feet scrubbed out our paths and wide steel mouths clamped onto and devoured our fragile landmarks. The faint traces of our being, our signatures to the world that we were here, at this place, were mangled. Distortion grew into chaos, and soon we recognized nothing of our beloved Greenfields.

They were gone in one agonizing week. Gone — leaving us with wide shallows in the grassless earth. Mounds of hard clay and stretches of ankle deep sand covered or replaced our sacred hideouts. Afterwards, we could only guess at where our tunnels and club houses had been. And in our minds, we placed grotesque trees at unreal angles against a wide, flat sky and searched desperately for the tree houses.

Afterwards we became a hot, tired band of restless hostiles with pernicious cloaks drawn tight about our small bones. We heard that they were going to build houses on our Greenfields. That's what Mr. Lawrence said, and Mr. Lawrence knew everything.

Still, we scampered over the clay hills and trudged through the sand. We continued at play long after the shallows had filled with oil-slick water. We watched the trucks dump discarded items from a civilization we never knew. Some of us got sick from eating the candy bars that would appear in heaps in the rubble. The girls would delight in collecting boxes of lipstick only to find that it caused sores. We forgot about Greenfields. This once sacred spot had acquired a new name. We called it — *"The Dump."*

Later, still, we would remember that our trees were gone, and then, we would remember how much we loved the berry-laden thickets and the moist, black earth. It became impossible for us to assemble things, to make some kind of picture of what our lives should be like. The only things we could think about, without effort, were the plush grasses and the sun-soaked tree tops. Our minds rested in these plush grasses, dark and steaming.

* * *

No one told us. They just arrived one afternoon, disinterested men in red fire trucks wearing long, black, rubber boots. We had somehow gathered without benefit of the spoken word; as if drawn by some magical drum beating out its haunting booms upon our tainted ether. It had been raining hard and long earlier during the week. It was raining then — a cold frightening rain that came from the south in dense patterns of needle sharp strands. The shallows of our extinct forest were full of clay colored water and the darting rain kept them in constant agitation. The oil slicks were broken by this tedious patter and sent flecks of blue, yellow, and green colors twinkling across the surface. Suddenly, the rain stopped, and a booming sun signaled our worst fears.

Hooks were in his chest and thighs when they pulled him up. Dennis Miller had drowned in the shallows. They built the houses years later. Mr. Lawrence — *knew everything.*

* * *

Winter Reprieve

**by
Lafayette King**

Mattie sat quietly by the fireplace as she removed the tattered pages of multicolored stationery from a ragged shoe box to look at them, and to read them once more as she often did as part of her nightly routine before retiring. Some of the letters were from the best stationery shops in Detroit, while others were written on scratch paper — one on a paper bag. All were tied together in bundles with twine that, years ago, the man who bought the ice for the icebox had left. She had collected the twine and used it to carefully tie the letters together. Then, she had put them neatly away in her timeworn box.

Where are those rascals? she wondered. *Surely, they could have called me by now to let me know what they are going to do for the holidays.*

Christmas was only two days away, and the fact that she had not heard a word from her children bothered Mattie much more than she was willing to admit under normal circumstances. But with Christmas getting closer, she was getting worried. She rarely imposed upon their time or activities, and usually she didn't ask for much. About the most she hoped for was to have them with her and around her to celebrate Christ's birthday. Without them there, it would be a truly lonely Christmas.

She was lonely now, and although they were a poor substitute, the letters with their captured memories helped to fill the void in her life. The fact that several of them brought back unpleasant or even painful memories did not matter, for even that was better than the emptiness that pestered her, and crowded in and around her weary seventy-two-year-old body like some cantankerous, old buzzard.

Carefully, she untied a bundle and selected one of the letters to read. It was one from her son, written when he was a student in medical school. He had wrote to ask her for more money so that he could move off campus into his own apartment, explaining that even though he was working part-time, he was still a little short of the security deposit. Could she help?

She remembered the occasion quite clearly and she felt her eyes becoming liquid. Her sister had been ill at the time, and all the extra money that she had managed to save had gone to assist her with her medical bills. There were trips back and forth to the doctors and medicines of all descriptions, none of which seemed to help. Finally, her sister died — died of cancer.

Burial expenses took the rest of the money she had saved, and she was forced to take a job as a janitress cleaning office buildings at night until she was eligible for her pension. She thought about her son, how he had ignored her and her problems, never once offering to assist when he knew that there was no one else she could call on. If her man had lived, things would have been a lot different, she was sure. Jake would have been a great help to her. But, he too, was gone — the victim of a fall from a scaffold on the building site of the People Mover.

She read further, "Mother, I don't like living on campus anymore," he stated in the letter. "I want to have my own place. I think I can handle it."

My, my, Mattie said to herself, *How insensitive children can be.* No consideration for anyone or the circumstances. He had a full scholarship with room and board, and still he wasn't satisfied. Just simply, "I want." *Well . . . there wasn't any money at the time — not one red cent*, she said to herself as she felt a tear chase itself down her flushed cheeks.

The fire crackled suddenly and interrupted Mattie's thoughts. She glanced up to check it, watching while the flames licked at the logs, and wondering if she would have enough firewood to last the winter, one which was becoming more severe by the day.

Her children had spent last Christmas with her, but they had not arrived until late Christmas Eve. Maybe, that was what they had in mind again this year. She hoped so, even though she would have preferred they come a few days earlier. She would not complain. She would be satisfied with that.

Mattie refolded her son's letter, put it back in its envelope, and selected another. This one brought a smile to her tired eyes. It was from her daughter, Stephanie, just before she had her first baby, Mattie's granddaughter, Rose.

The letter began, "Mama, the baby is due soon and I need you with me when it comes. I am scared to death. Please come. I miss you so much, Mama." Another tear fell from her chin, but this time, the tears she shed were tears of joy. She had been so happy and thankful that her first grandchild had been born healthy, crying and screaming like a little, adorable banshee. That day was probably one of the most wonderful days of her life.

All in all, she supposed, her children had turned out o.k. They had not become criminals or degenerates. They were both sane, productive, individuals who, in the end, made her feel proud with their accomplishments. Steven finished medical school and went to work in a large hospital in New York.

Stephanie, although she was divorced with one child, worked as a law clerk in Detroit for Wayne County about thirty miles away from her home in Belleville. Some of the blame for their callous attitude could probably be placed on the harsh times in which they were forced to live. With all the rushing around, and hustling, and bustling, they probably didn't have time left for themselves. And while the times were changing, and changing rapidly, her own life had remained relatively stable. For that, she was thankful.

It was almost 11:00 o'clock, and still no word from her dear children. Suddenly, the phone rang. It was Stephanie.

"Hi, mama," Stephanie yelled into the phone. "What are we having for Christmas dinner?"

"Hello, Stephanie . . .," Mattie replied, stalling for time. She had not even considered the possibility that she might have to cook. For some reason, she had assumed that the kids were going to bring dinner already prepared. Normally, she would have had something to fix in an emergency, but her food stamps were late coming — printing problems, she had been told. The only thing she had was some Polish sausage and a couple of food stamps left over from the previous month.

Mattie had an idea. If she used the last of her food stamps to get a jar of sauerkraut. Then, she could have . . . "Polish sausage, sauerkraut, and bread baked on the hearth," she yelled into the phone.

"That's a great idea," agreed Stephanie. "I was so hoping you would bake some bread. No one else in the world can bake bread the way you do."

"Well, I'll make sure there's plenty of it. Stephanie?"

"Yes, Mama?"

"Have you heard from your brother, Steve?"

"Not a word, mama. But, you know how Steve is about writing."

"I was just curious. That's all."

"Okay. Well, see you later, Mama." When Stephanie hung up, Mattie was a little disappointed in herself for not having used some forethought regarding the Christmas meal. The traditional dinner of turkey or ham with all the trimmings would be out for Mattie and her family this year. This year's meal, although simple and ordinary, would be special only because it would include her old fashioned, hearth baked bread — the type that both of her children adored. And it would even be more special because she and her children would be together again, and united in fellowship — she hoped.

The winter wind howled around the little shack in which Mattie lived. A little concerned, Mattie took the poker and stirred the red hot embers until the fire crackled and popped. Then, she placed several logs on top and watched while the flames licked and leaped, turning the logs black, and sending small puffs of smoke scurrying up the chimney.

When she finished she slipped quickly into her nightgown, then walked to the window and peeked out. *Looks like a storm is brewing,* she said to herself as she turned and went into her bedroom.

She was pulling the covers back, when she noticed that a letter had fallen between the night stand and the bed. She picked it up and added it to the others in the box. Then, she climbed into bed where she waited patiently for sleep.

She shivered. It was winter, and bitter cold. Except for the holiday season, she didn't care for winter so much anymore. For it was during this mean season of the year that so many of her friends had left her over the years past. Some had left while trying to do just the simplest things — things that they had done all their lives, like shoveling snow, walking to the market, or trying to cut their own kindling and firewood, and some, seemingly, just crawled into their beds and never, never woke up.

But then, too, there were the good times like the sleigh rides that she and her sister had gone on, hot apple cider with cinnamon sticks — her Uncle Luke, drunk with wine, falling on the slippery ice. She also remembered visits to the farm in Alberta where her grandmother was always busy in the kitchen canning and baking goodies like sweet potato pies and coconut cakes. There would be turnip and mustard greens with ham hocks cooking on the stove. Those were festive times — simple, endearing, and uncomplicated.

* * *

The next morning, Christmas eve, Mattie was up early. The first thing she did after dressing for the cold was to go out and get more wood for the fire. She placed another log in the fireplace, then stood near it a moment to warm the blood in her frail, but still active body.

A few minutes later, she put a second wrap around her head, got her special snow walking cane, and set out laboriously for Paul Johnson's General Store, a distance that seemed to be getting longer with each passing day. Sometimes, she wondered if old man Johnson was moving his store on purpose, just to make her walk.

"Good morning Mattie," Mr. Johnson spoke almost cheerily. "What is an old gal like you doing out on a day like this — don't you know that's bad for your health?"

"I know, Paul, but the kids are coming and I need to cook something for Christmas."

"Well, you won't get to cook nothin', if you dead in your grave. So, what can I get for you, a ham or one of these fat turkey hens?"

"Just a jar of sauerkraut, will do," Mattie replied as she reached her shaking hands into her purse and took out the last of her food stamps.

"Sauerkraut? Now, Mattie that won't make no proper Christmas dinner?"

"I'm afraid it will have to do, Paul. These two food stamps are all I have left."

"Well, give them here," Mr. Johnson said with a degree of irritation that embarrassed Mattie and caused her to drop her head and pretend to study her hands.

"Mattie?"

"Yes, Paul?" Mattie replied trying to avoid Mr. Johnson's eyes.

"Merry Christmas. You take this turkey home and cook those kids a proper meal."

"Oh no, Paul . . . really, you don't have to do that."

"Gal, I know that. I was going to do it, anyway. You just saved me a trip down to your place."

"Paul, I don't know how I can ever thank you."

"You don't have to. Just you take your time and get home safe now, and when you get there, you stay there."

"Thank you, Paul, and a blessed Merry Christmas to you."

"And, I put your sauerkraut in the bag, too," Mr. Johnson yelled as she left.

"Thank you, Paul." Mattie said, waving good bye as she stepped out into the brisk air filled with light flurries of snow.

When Mattie returned home, she was filled with unbridled joy. *The Lord will make a way — won't He*, she said to herself as she sat about immediately to dress and slow cook the turkey. She would cook the sauerkraut and sausage on Christmas morning.

Early that afternoon, the phone rang loudly, almost jumping off the kitchen wall. She rushed to answer it.

"Hi, mom, it's me, Steven."

"Hi, son. What are you doing? Where are you — you coming home for Christmas?"

"Well, mom, that's why I called. It seems I won't be able to make it. They put me on on-call duty over Christmas, and I have an emergency, fourteen hour, very complicated, surgical procedure scheduled for tonight. There is no way that I can get there."

"Well, I understand, son," Mattie replied, trying not to show the true depths of her disappointment. "I would love to have you here, but not at the expense of someone's life. You stay, and do what you can. Say a prayer, and let the Lord guide your hands."

"Thanks, mom. I'll do the best I can, and if at all possible, maybe I can get to visit you before new year."

"Okay, son. Just come, whenever you can."

The rest of the day passed uneventfully. By 9:00 p.m., the turkey and bread had been baked, the fire set for the night, and Mattie was tired, so she retired.

Trying to get to sleep, however, turned into quite a chore for Mattie, primarily, because of Steven's disappointing telephone call. There was no one on this earth who could know how much she truly wanted to be with her family on this particular Christmas — more than any other Christmas in her life. Maybe, she supposed, it was because of her age and her knowing full well that tomorrow was not promised to anyone.

Several hours passed while Mattie hung in limbo. Finally, she decided to get up and put some extra wood on the fire to insure its chances of surviving until morning.

When she completed her task, she climbed back into bed and snuggled deep beneath her quilted covers, praying that the snow wouldn't be knee-deep by morning so that she could go out into the woods and gather more firewood. Moments later, she was fast asleep.

* * *

Suddenly, something woke Mattie and she sat up with a start. She glanced over at the large clock near her bed. It was after 4:00 a.m. Then, she thought she heard a light tap at the door. She turned her ear and listened, intently. There was nothing. She had just about decided that it was the wind when someone pounded on her door loudly. *Who in the world is out this time of night,* she wondered as she got up, picked up her afghan from the chair, and threw it around her shoulders. Then, she went to her window and peeked out, curiously. Standing in her doorway, she saw a tall, shadowy figure in the dark, holding a large box, wrapped in shiny paper with a large red bow around it.

Mattie didn't recognize the man, and suddenly, she was frightened. "Be gone, or I'll call the police," she yelled. "I haven't ordered anything."

The gaunt figure shouted, "Mom, it's me, Steven."

At the sound of his voice, Mattie's mood changed, instantly. "Lord, Lord!" she said loudly with excitement. "Is that you, Steven?"

"Yeah, it's me, mom."

Tears of joy filled Mattie's eyes as she rushed to open the door. "Steven, Steven!" she said, as her son hustled in from the cold and slammed the door closed behind him.

"Hi, mom. Man, I tell you, it's cold out there. Here, I brought something for you."

"Put it down somewhere, son. I'm just happy to see you. I thought you weren't going to make it!"

"I know, mom, but at the last minute, a co-worker of mine volunteered to take my place. And, here I am!"

"The Lord will make a way — won't He?" Mattie said as she embraced her son.

"Yes, He will," Steven agreed. "Here, mom. It's a present for you. Something, I hope you will like."

"I'm sure I will, Steve, but put it down, and let me hang up your coat."

Steven sat the box on the floor, then removed his cashmere overcoat and handed it to Mattie who, in turn, hung it in the hall closet.

"Lord, just let me look at you," she said as she leaned back and scrutinized her son. "You're too thin. You're working too hard — and why don't you write me anymore?" she scolded.

"Well, Mom," Steven began, "I'm so busy doing surgery and writing reports that I don't write anymore than I have to. I can't even stand the sight of a pen — and how have you been, Mother, dear?" Steve asked, changing the subject.

"O.K., I guess. Nothing more than general, old age, aches and pains. Have a seat by the fire in my old, comfort chair and rest yourself awhile. I'll heat you some tea."

"Have you heard from Stephanie?" Steven asked as Mattie hung the water kettle over the hearth.

"Night before last. They're fine. Said she would be

here bright and early this morning. I can't wait to see Rose. That little babe is a real card. She is going to be quite a character when she grows up."

"Well, I wouldn't count on it. The roads between here and the airport were super bad. I almost didn't make it in my little rental car — had to detour several times on my way here tonight. If it gets any worse, all the roads between here and Detroit will be closed by morning."

Mattie went to the window and looked out. Sure enough it was still snowing, and she knew her son was right. "Well, as bad as it looks, I sure hope she doesn't attempt to drive in it. At this rate, it will be knee deep by morning for sure."

"Maybe, you should try and call."

"I think I will," Mattie said as she went to the phone and dialed. She waited. A moment later, a computer voice stated, "Sorry for this inconvenience, but services have been temporarily disrupted due to weather."

"What happened?" asked Steven.

"I didn't get her. The lines are down, but I sure wish I knew if she was alright."

When the water was hot, Mattie made two cups of steaming, hot tea that she and Steven drank while sitting close to the fire and conversing quietly. Moments later, Steven had dozed off into deep sleep.

While her son slept, Mattie got up, tiptoed over to her present, and opened it like a mischievous kid on Christmas morning. It was a brand new electric space heater. Although she was delighted, she knew it would never replace her hearth. *Well, you can't bake no bread on it — can you?*

While Mattie waited for the light of day worrying about her daughter, she put the sausage and sauerkraut in an old iron pot and hung it over her hearth. Then, she sat back down in her rocking chair beside Steven and rested her eyes.

Sometime later, the rapid beeping of a car horn shook Mattie awake. Hurriedly, she raced to the window and looked out to see her daughter Stephanie and her granddaughter Rose climbing out of a car, hanging from the back of a tow truck, loaded down with presents.

"Lord, you will make a way — won't you!" she screamed as she rushed to the door.

So, Mattie's dearest wish became a reality. Her children had come to visit her for Christmas *Tide* and she was happy. There indeed, had been a reprieve of winter, a brief break in the low hanging clouds that permitted a small ray of sunlight to enter her modest abode and fill her life with the joys of celebration on this, the Christ Child's birthday.

* * *

He Was Magnificent

Joe Louis Barrow
   he was born.
From fields of Alabama
   to streets of Detroit.

Within infinity of a galaxy, did they know a streaking star would cross their path. Sparkling across the sky, the world took notice.

Tame and hushed, till he climbed through
   ring of rope, floor of canvas.

Unchained . . . unshackled . . . unleashed.
The force exploded on all those who stood before it.
   pounded
   slammed
   battered
   they all fell, and saluted his might.

You showed em Joe . . . you showed em what a man, a black man could do. Even within confines of a roped square.

As shadows
   We were there with him, as he loomed over crippled foes being counted out.

As a beacon
   black faces turned to him. He kept heads afloat amidst overflowing dregs of bigotry.

No one can splinter the boulder of your greatness.
No one can mirror the reflection of your feats.

Joe Louis
    the brown bomber, champion, hero.
        There were none like you before, and none after.

By Thomas Lewis
© 1985
Through Ebony Eyes

* * *

A Fantasy

by
Ruth Rosa Green

On a beautiful mid-August afternoon, I boarded the cruise ship, "Madonna," bound for Saussan in the Mahamba Islands. It was my first cruise and I was like a child filled with excitement and wonder. As the boat shoved off, I had a feeling that I was embarking upon a new and unforgettable adventure.

For a long time I remained at the rail, lost in my thoughts, and watching the harbor fade into the distance. The call for dinner sounded, and I hurried anxiously to savor the cuisine that I had heard so much about.

Upon finishing an enjoyable and delicious dinner of fresh seafood dishes with all the trimmings, I took a stroll on the deck to get my sea legs. I circled the deck twice, then stopped and leaned against the rail to watch the golden sun fill the horizon as it expanded and disappeared from view. Below, I could hear the waves splashing against the hull as the ship skimmed through the water. I turned around and sat on one of the empty deck lounge chairs, relaxing and enjoying the cool sea breeze that playfully tugged at my skirts. Stars suddenly began to appear in the beautiful, clear, blue sky, and soon the whole sky was filled with tiny, dancing lights. Amidst all of this peacefulness, I could hear the ship's orchestra playing the melodious strains of "Moonlight Serenade" in the main ballroom. I had wanted to stay longer, but the day had been tiring. So, with a feeling of warm contentment, I retired to my cabin for the night.

A week later, I awoke one morning to find that we had already docked at Andross Island. The Captain announced that we would be there for a few hours before sailing on to our destination, the Mahamba Islands.

When I got to the main deck, some of the passengers had already disembarked. Hurriedly, I went to the dining room, had a quick continental breakfast, then went ashore to do some exploring on my own.

My curiosity had peaked when the Captain told us, the night before, that Andross was the largest island in the Mahamba chain. His vivid description of the island with its sparsely populated, white, sandy beaches, and tiny villages nestled among lush greenery, filled me with anxiety. He also mentioned, however, that we would not get to visit the eastern coast where the second largest barrier reef on earth was located.

As I walked farther and farther from the dock into the interior of the island, I became more attuned to the breathless and endless beauty all around me. Before I realized it, I was standing on the face of a hill covered with thick green grass, shrubs, flowers, and majestic trees that stood with outstretched arms, shading and protecting all that came within their domain. Above, beautiful exotic birds sang and flittered from tree to tree — and in the distance, other hills, lagoons, and valleys, all around, as far as the eyes could see. I was overwhelmed.

Suddenly, the ship's horn bellowed. Quickly, I glanced at my watch and panicked. It was one-thirty. I had been gone for two hours. The ship was scheduled to depart at two o'clock, and since I had wandered so far into the interior of the island, I knew there was no way I could get back to the dock before it sailed. Still, I felt that I had to try. So, I grabbed up my purse and started the long journey back to the dock. I was about half way there, breathless, my neck rubbed raw by my camera strap, when I heard the ships farewell blasts. Realizing that my efforts were useless, I gave up, slowed my pace, and wandered into the harbor village, tired, and thoroughly embarrassed by my stupidity.

So, there I was, a young, inexperienced, starry-eyed, bachelor-girl, stranded on a strange island, alone, with no one to turn to, and no knowledge of the native language or customs. I was frightened. With a deep sigh and a determination to make the best of a bad situation, I decided that I needed to find a place to stay, and a job until the ship returned and I could get home.

I saw a bar. It looked friendly, so I wandered inside, somewhat timidly. Standing at the far end of the room behind the bar, I saw the profile of a tall, slender, blond-haired, pleasant looking man who appeared to be in his early thirties. As I walked toward him, he turned around, looked up with his dancing blue eyes, smiled, and started walking toward me, his right hand extended in a gesture of friendliness.

"Hello," he said. "My name is Tom, the owner of this establishment. May I help you?"

With a sigh of relief at hearing someone who spoke English, I smiled and answered, "Hello. Yes, I hope you can." I told him that my name was Elizabeth, that I was from the ship, "Madonna," and had been exploring the island when the ship left me behind; that I needed a place to stay, and a job until the ship returned.

After listening to my story, Tom willingly agreed to provide me with both, a job and a place to stay. My stomach growled, and he asked if I was hungry. "Well, not really," I answered, not wanting to push my good fortune. He sort of chuckled as if he knew I was lying, then directed me to sit at one of the tables. Weary and tired, I quickly sat down and kicked off my shoes. Moments later, I was devouring a delicious meal of some tasteful, exotic, island dishes.

Afterwards, Tom showed me to my room. I was so tired, that I fell asleep as soon as my head hit the pillow.

I was awakened the next morning by the sound of singing birds. Drowsily, I looked out the window and saw that the sun was high in the sky. I had slept well past breakfast. Checking the clock on the table beside my bed proved my calculation correct. It was 11:45 a.m. As I was hurriedly preparing to go downstairs, there was a knock on the door. Opening the door and saying, "Come in," at the same time, I was startled to see Tom standing there with a breakfast tray.

"Good morning," he said as he sat the tray on the table by an open window. "I thought we could discuss your problems over a little breakfast, if you don't mind."

I nodded, smiled, and said, "Thanks, I think that's a great idea."

It was decided that I would stay in this room at the hotel and work as long as I chose to stay. During our conversation, Tom told me how he had come to be in Andross.

He was a wealthy orphan from Rhode Island, whose yacht had been shipwrecked near the island while on a deep-sea fishing trip several years earlier. Almost at the point of death, he and his crew were rescued by some of the younger men from the island.

Tom was given to an old, motherless woman who nursed and cared for him until he recovered. "Old Trinella" adopted him as her own and loved him dearly until her death two years before.

Tom recovered from his wounds, but chose to remain on the lovely, peaceful island, where no forms of prejudice existed. His surviving crew, however, returned to the states.

In time, Tom learned the customs and language of these people and gained their love, respect, and friendship. During the process, he met, fell in love with, and married a beautiful island girl, whose name was Mala. But, his happiness was short lived, Mala died while giving birth to a lovely daughter and there was much sadness for a long time in the family.

As was the custom of this island, the baby was cared for and raised by her female relatives in her grandfather, "Old Ken's," home. Tom visited his lovely daughter as frequently as he could. But, because of his daughter Mala's untimely death, "Old Ken" hated Tom, and his visits had to be made in secret.

From a picture Tom showed me, I could see that the child's complexion was a combination of rose and gold, and her name was Golden Rose. Her beautiful round, dark eyes were set in an angelic face with a tiny pointed nose, and a bow-shaped mouth. Blue-black silken hair hung below her shoulders. She appeared to be a happy, carefree, and lovable child.

One day I wandered further than usual on my daily walk, from the hotel and suddenly found myself looking into a large clearing with an enormous white house in the center, surrounded by trees and flowers, in a well-sculptured garden with three small pools of water. In one of the pools I saw a little girl about four years old, splashing and playing.

The water was a magnificent blue with flecks of sunlight shimmering and dancing over it and the child. Nearby, sat two doting females, watching the child very carefully. Instinctively, I knew this was Tom's Golden Rose.

As I watched the lovely innocence of this child at play, I was suddenly startled when she shrieked with glee, jumped from the pool, and raced toward an approaching man. As the man came closer, I recognized her father, Tom. Both were running toward each other with outstretched arms. He lovingly gathered his daughter's wet body to his breast, kissing her, laughing, and chattering all at the same time.

My admiration for him seemed to increase alarmingly at the sight of such a touching scene. Feeling like a spy, an intruder, I quietly crept away and slowly sauntered back to the hotel. My thoughts were filled with love and emotional happiness for Tom and the undeniable bond that existed between him and his daughter, and yet, saddened, because I was unable to share their joy.

Being a young, attractive, black woman from the states where racial prejudices were prevalent, I became frustrated with the acknowledgment that I was desperately in love with this attractive, tall, slender, blond, blued-eyed widower — someone, I was sure, who thought of me only as a friend.

I had long ago fallen in love with the island, its people, lifestyle, peace, and tranquility. After a week of being exposed to all that the island had to offer, I had decided to make Andross my new home.

* * *

Two months passed, and the rainy season began. A strong wind started blowing, banging the window shutters against the sides of the hotel. Shadowy, grotesque figures from the plants and trees danced on the walls in the empty, dimly-lit bar, sending shivering chills through my body.

Suddenly, the front door swung open and a tall, slender figure, dressed in black with long, gray hair hanging to his shoulders, burst into the room. It was "Old Ken," Golden Rose's grandfather — drunk, full of rage, and brandishing a machete which reflected flashes of lightening into the darkened room.

"Where is that murderer of my Mala?" he called out angrily. "Tom. Tom, where you hiding? You die, this time. You killed my daughter, Mala. Now, you die!"

Petrified with fear, I somehow managed to call out, "Tom is not here, please go away!"

"Old Ken" ignored me and stumbled down the hall into another room. I was still standing behind the bar frightened and unable to move. Tom came in from the kitchen, and quickly pulled me to the floor behind the bar, saying, "Stay quiet, and stay down! Old Ken will go away soon. It's the whiskey talking. Every time there is a storm, he gets drunk and threatens to kill me."

Unable to contain my love and fear for his life any longer, I began to cry. Between tears and sobs, I confessed my love for him and his beautiful Golden Rose. All the while he was holding me in his arms, listening to me, telling me not to cry, and that he loved me, too. Then, he kissed me, quieting my sobs, and holding me closer in his arms. We could hear Old Ken going from room to room slamming doors, overturning furniture, and still calling for Tom. Finally, he came down the hallway and past the bar, cursing and mumbling as he staggered out of the front door and into the rage of the storm.

Oblivious to our surroundings and thrilled with the ecstasy of our newly declared love, we made love where we were, on the floor, with an intensity that matched that of the storm, glorying in blissful oneness of body and soul.

After what seemed to be hours, physically exhausted, but more fulfilled than words can express, we lay silently happy in a warm and everlasting embrace of tenderness.

Suddenly realizing that the storm was over, we dressed, and walked out the front door to the freshness of a cool, refreshing pre-dawn. Crossing the porch to the steps, we saw Old Ken lying on his stomach. He was so still, his body soaked from the rain. Looking closer, we saw that he was dead, the blade of the huge knife was buried in his abdomen. Apparently, he had stumbled on the steps, falling on his machete in the process.

After the nightmare of it all, I met Golden Rose and her relatives. When they were told of our love, I was welcomed with open arms and preparations began for our wedding. The burning of flat, round candles was the first and most important part of many ceremonies before any wedding.

On the evening of the "Candle Ceremony," for no apparent reason, I began to feel edgy. At the beginning of sunset, some of the young men, seated in a large circle, started to play native love songs on their instruments. This was the signal for the bride and groom to be to make their entrance. Two seats had been placed on a raised platform, covered with island flowers, partially inside of the circle. Directly, at the opposite end of the circle was a table lined with coconut halves filled with oil. These were to be lit by the couple with an ancient ceremonial torch presented to them by the High Priest.

Tom entered the circle from the right side, dressed in a white shirt and white trousers with a lei of red flowers around his neck. I was dressed in a white dress, and also wore a lei of red flowers. My entrance into the circle was from the left side. We met in the center of the circle, joined hands, and walked to the table to receive the ceremonial torch. We were within a few steps of the torch when I tripped and fell . . . .

Suddenly, I sat up, shook my head, and looked around in disbelief. Slowly, I recognized my surroundings. I looked beside me, and there was my dear husband sleeping soundly. Still half asleep, I got up and went to check on the children in their rooms. They too, were sound asleep. Satisfied that everyone was safe, and all was secure, I climbed back into bed and snuggled deeply beneath the covers. It had all been just a dream. Even though it was, I was still filled with many warm thoughts.

I counted my many blessings, and dreamed no more that night.

* * *

Judgment Day on South Street

by
Herbert R. Metoyer, Jr.

This is a short, humorous, fictitious story about a Chevrolet Sedan and its role in judgment day on South Street. The story is based on an actual incident that occurred in 1943, in a little southern town by the name of Oakdale. The names of the characters were changed to protect the innocent and the guilty alike. I hope you find the story interesting . . . .

* * *

In May 1943, I was eight years old, in the fourth grade. It was a hot, humid night. The only kind you would expect to find in Louisiana at the start of the summer.

We lived in an old house of very modest standards that grew as our family grew. My much younger brother, Bryford, and I shared a single twin bed in a back room beneath a tin roof. Although it could get quite hot there during the summer months, it was one of the best places in the world to hibernate during a thunder shower. On such occasions, I would spend many pleasurable hours there, reading, and listening to the many random, rhythmic patterns of the rain.

The walls of the room where my brother and I slept were covered with a variety of old newspapers. In addition to being highly decorative, they also served as insulation during the winter, and a mosquito barrier during the summer. My favorite comics,

"Prince Valiant" and "Flash Gordon," graced positions of eminence above the head of our bed.

I usually wasted several hours of sleep trying to make sure that my brother stayed on his side during the night. Most of the time, I was unsuccessful. I slept on my back. My brother was a side sleeper. His favorite position was the "fetal curl" with his feet and legs thrown awkwardly toward my side of the bed. So, I would lie there, waiting in the night, like a spider watching his prey, just waiting for him to move one inch toward my side. And when he did, I would take my left foot with extreme prejudice, and joust him back onto his.

Now, don't get me wrong. It was not a matter of me not wanting my brother to touch me. There was, however, another matter of greater significance. My brother occasionally wet the bed. Because I was twice his size, he would naturally gravitate to my side during the night. In the mornings, we would wake up arguing about who wet who. Since the evidence was almost always on my side of the bed, you can see that I was usually in an untenable position.

Worst yet, was when this would happen during the winter. We had a potbellied, wood heater that my mother kept burning during the day until we went to bed. On those cold nights, when he would wet, we would have to lie there freezing in it until she got up the next morning and started a new fire.

Anyway, while we were still jockeying for position at about 1:30 a.m., I had no idea that Judgment Day had arrived on South Street.

On this street, lived some of the finest citizens in our little black, southern community. Each, you might say, a pillar of the society.

Mr. and Mrs. Sudds, my sister Delores' godparents,

lived on the east side of the street. We all referred to them as *Marraine and Parraine,* creole for Godmother and Godfather. Parraine, who some folks considered a little too uppity, ran a small grocery store and filling station of the hand pump variety. His wife was a school teacher in the Hardwood Quarters, a sawmill housing project across town.

Across the street from them lived the McWilliams family with their four beautiful daughters (one of whom was the apple of my eye at the time) and son, little McWilliams, Junior.

Down the street, lived Mrs. Evelenor Lewis. Mrs. Lewis was the typical little old lady who had raised hell all her life, then in her later years, to atone for her sins, she preached "Hell and Damnation" to everyone else in town. Her unofficial position as a "Saver of Souls" gave her license to meddle in everyone's affairs, and she did this on a more than frequent basis.

The rest of the people on the street, like Jessie Bell, JuJu Joe, Delafosse, and others, were neither overly religious or sinful. Just ordinary people, who did ordinary things.

This was true for everyone, I guess, except "Bulldog." Everyone swore Bulldog was the worst sinner in town. Although Bulldog never bothered anyone, he was prone to sip liberally and frequently from a bottle of Elderberry wine that he carried in his back pocket for this purpose. Frankly, most of the time he was drunk — surrounded by that mystic aroma of liquor and urine that usually identified persons of his persuasion.

In those days, we all had "outhouses." A storm blew Bulldog's over and he never did set it back upright. I don't know where he went for his more serious toilet duties, but I do know that at any time, he was subject to come out on his front porch in full view of anyone and relieve his bladder on a half-dead rose bush that his deceased wife had once planted.

In Oakdale, there weren't many blacks who could afford to own an automobile. Most of them had mules or bicycles. A few had old, antique jalopies or trucks that rattled up and down the dusty streets when they were dry, or churned the mud when they were wet. This being the case, there were not many of them who understood fully how the newer vehicles functioned.

My parents did not own a vehicle of any type, except the bicycle my father rode to work. Mr. McWilliams did. He had just bought a brand new, used, baby blue Chevrolet sedan. Of course, this elevated his social position in the community to a new height with friends and neighbors stopping by to congratulate him and admire his new car.

"Yeah-suh, Bro' Mac, you done yo self right proud this time."

"Yeah, a whole lot of them white folks ain't got no car like that'un you got."

"I don't know, Bro Mac, but if I was you, I wouldn't be driving that kar uptown cross them tracks — too much. Them Ku Kluxing Klan men might get mad — might think you poking fun at 'em."

"Yeah, you know they can't stand to see a black man what done got hisself somethin'."

"Ain't it the truth."

Of course, most of the excitement was enjoyed by the children who examined the car in detail, while laughing, playing, and begging for rides.

"Boy, bet that kar can go 300 miles an hour — dust'll be jes' flying."

"Ain't no kor go that fast."

"Well, I bet'ya it'll go more'n 200."

"Awww — you don't know nothin' what you talking 'bout. That ain't no spanking, brand new car nohow."

"Well, my daddy say — if he get that job at the mill over in Mabbs, he gon' get us one. And his gon' be better'n this'un."

To eliminate some of the congestion around his house, Mr. McWilliams would load the car full of kids and give them a ride around the quarters, stopping periodically to chase some of the older boys off his running boards.

So, on this particularly quiet summer night, about a week later, the stillness was shattered when the car horn started blasting away for no apparent reason.

The first person out of the house and into the street was Mrs. Evelenor Lewis. Scared out of her wits, she immediately started crying and shouting, "Oh, Lord! Oh, my Lord, it's Judgment Day! Gather up the sheep. The day of reckoning's here. Blessed be th' Lamb."

The horn blasting away and her crying and yelling, soon aroused everyone else. Sleepily, they came out, and without one question, assumed that Judgment Day was, in fact, upon them.

Mrs. Sudds, who was a very impressionable person, to say the least, soon had everybody marching around in a daisy-chain circle singing "Neer-row My God to Thee."

About halfway through the refrain, Mrs. Lewis decided to go back to her house and *will* away all of her worthless furniture and treasures. How this little old senior citizen, ninety to one hundred pounds at the most, was able to drag her furniture, including the couch, out onto her front porch, is still one of Oakdale's unsolved mysteries.

Talking to no-one in particular, she yelled, "Reverend Wieley, you gets my mother's Holy Bible and two of them guinney hens out back. The rest goes to my cousin Rochelle. Tell Ladybird, she can have my white, rabbit-coon, fur coat."

Then, down the street she yelled, "Mrs. Sudds you still want that yellow feather, Sunday-go-to-meeting hat I bought last summer?" . . . *The circle kept circling.*

Most of the larger kids were standing around, open mouthed, gazing up at the nighttime sky — waiting for some sort of apparition to appear. Some of the younger kids, who did not fully understand what was going on, were crying. Every dog in the neighborhood was up, howling and barking with one pup racing around, outside the circle, snapping at Mr. Sudds' flannel nightgown.

Bulldog, half-drunk, finally came out on his front porch to see what was going on and to tend his ablutions.

Spying him, Mrs. Lewis started shouting "Oh Lord, there's po' Bulldog . . . Lord hav' mercy on bro' Bulldog — your child of darkness. I done what I could for 'im, Lord — but, he been a'testing my Holy Spirit."

Then, down the street, she shouted, "Everybody stop the singing! Start up the Prayer Band and pray for po' Bulldog's soul, satan's straining on 'im right now — dragging him right straight down to the bottom of hell!"

To Bulldog she said, "Bulldog — fall down on thy knees, cast away thy sinful ways, and throw thyself down on the mer-cey of the Lord." Then she did the "Sanctified Foot Stomp" *(jumping up and down while clapping her hands)* and shouted, "Hallay-lew-ya! My God's a forgiving Gawd . . . ."

Bulldog, not ever really looking up, finished shaking his spigot, mumbled "Ole Bitch," then turned and staggered back into his little shotgun shack . . . *The circle kept circling.*

Little McWilliams, Junior, who had been standing in the front yard during most of the commotion, finally noticed that it was the car horn blowing. It took him, however, several trips around the outside of the circle shouting, "Daddy, Daddy! Dat's dat car hone' blowing," before he was finally able to get his father's attention. Abruptly — the circle stopped, almost as if someone had suddenly stuck a pole into the spokes of a fast moving bicycle.

After a few moments of milling around, several of the adults followed the boy across the yard to the car. Sure enough, it was the car horn — still blasting away.

The situation, however, was still far from being resolved. Since no one present knew anything about cars, there followed an impromptu brainstorming session to determine the best way to stop the horn from blowing. And since the key was not in the car, and the switch was already off, someone suggested throwing water on it.

"Well, I don't know about that," Bro' Mac said, more than just a little skeptical, "I don't wanna go chunking water on it and mess-up somethin'."

"Well, ya got to do something, Bro' Mac," JuJu Joe pleaded, "It's been squawking like that most a hour now and hit ain't let up none, yet."

"Shootz, we could be standing out c'here all night."

"Now, ain't that the truth."

"Well, I don't know about y'all, but I needs to get myself some sleep fo' that sun come up. I got to go 'cross them tracks and hang out Mis' Vidrine's washing in the morning," Jessie Bell stated as she folded her arms and rared back, quite disgusted with the whole situation.

Now, Bro' Mac loved his car, dusted and polished it religiously every evening before he retired. He, naturally, was deeply concerned. But, for lack of a better idea, and to keep the peace among his neighbors, he reluctantly lifted the hood while the rest formed a haphazard bucket brigade. At his signal, they feverishly started pitching water on the engine. Finally, the battery ran down and the horn died a slow painful death . . . .

Unnoticed until now — the lightning bugs, for some reason, seemed to be lighting up the whole sky.

Needless to say, there were some mighty embarrassed folks standing around in the mud and water, fanning away lightning bugs and slapping at mosquitoes. Not only were they embarrassed in front of each other, but they were anticipating the even greater embarrassment that would result if the rest of Oakdale found out about the incident.

So, to circumvent this, they gathered all the children together and dared them with threats on their lives, if they told another living soul about what had transpired.

The matter settled, they each filtered back into their respective homes — ignoring the pleas of Mrs. Lewis, who called for someone to come and help move her furniture back into her house.

Since the black quarters in Oakdale were pretty small, many of the people on the adjacent streets had heard the commotion. Most of them thought someone had died. The next morning at school, the teachers were especially anxious to find out what had happened on South street. Naturally, they asked the children who lived there. All disavowed any knowledge. This only served to incite my grandmother's curiosity all the more.

My grandmother, Mrs. Edna C. Glenn, taught the fourth grade. She was a formidable woman, who was an expert in the efficient use of an 18-inch ruler. It served as a ruler, a swagger stick, a blackboard pointer, and when the situation dictated, it served as an exceptional tool for "tanning" little black bottoms.

So, with that introduction to my grandmother, you can understand the concern that Boo-Boo (one of my classmates) displayed when she directed him, sternly, to the cloakroom. With ruler in hand, she demanded that he tell her what happened on South street. We all feared for Boo-Boo's life and were quite surprised to hear my grandmother's laughter pierce the silence.

With tears rolling down her chubby cheeks, she stumbled out of the cloakroom hanging onto the walls for support. She then called Mrs. Simpson and Mrs. Benson, the third and fifth grade teachers, over. Back to the cloakroom they went. There was more laughter and more tears.

Boo-Boo, who had started to enjoy his new found popularity, spared none of the details.

This went on all morning long with different teachers trooping in and out the cloak room to hear a firsthand account of the episode.

Needless to say, the day was half spent before things returned to normal — all because of "Judgment Day on South Street."

* * *

A Letter to William

**by
Peggy A. Moore**

During World War II — back in the early 1940's, I lived with my family in an all-colored section of Detroit, a large, Northern American city. I was eleven years old at that time and attended a segregated school nestled amid a sprawling factory complex that belched smoke and hissed noise twenty-four hours a day.

It was a time like we'll never see again. Huge factories that once turned out classy cars for the well-to-do, transformed overnight into ones that built weapons of war. And as fast as they came off the conveyor belts and assembly lines, they were shipped to Europe and other far away places like Guam and Guadacanal in the South Pacific.

My father, Benjamin, a big, dark-complexioned man who stood over six-feet-tall, worked two shifts at two different factories as did most of the men who lived in our tightly knitted community. My father hadn't been called to serve his country because he had this condition the doctors labeled — *rheumatic heart disease.* Whatever that was, it didn't slow him any at all and he never once missed a day at work.

I could always tell when he was at home because the aroma of the Cuban cigars he smoked, seeped into every room of our modest, six-room, rented house. "Ruth Ann, Ruth Ann," he would yell to me as his large frame bustled through the screen door off the back porch, "Bring me that big pitcher of lemonade from the icebox, 'cause I'm going to drink every drop." Then, he would laugh a laugh that could be heard clear to the end of our block. I would rush, get the frosty pitcher, and hand it to him just as he plopped down in his overstuffed, easy chair in our parlor.

My mother, Anna Mae, had creamy skin, the color of fresh buttermilk, and jet-black hair that was smooth and soft to the touch as silk. Although she was a small woman who barely stood five-feet tall, she was truly a giant in every other respect.

Each afternoon around three o'clock, you'd find Anna Mae outside of the factory gate waiting anxiously for my father, Benjamin, with a brown paper lunch bag in her hand. Promptly at three-thirty, the old factory whistle would blow, signaling the end of the daytime shift. Anna Mae would scan the mass of human, sweating flesh that poured out through the plant gates until she caught sight of her Benjamin. Then, she would rush up to him, kiss his covered-with-grease cheeks, hand him his lunch — then, wave good-bye as he boarded the streetcar that would take him across town to work yet another eight-hour shift.

With Benjamin on his way, Anna Mae would stand watching the congested, swaying, squealing streetcar until it was well out of sight. Then, she would smooth her neatly starched, cotton house dress down with the flats of her hands, toss her head high, and head for home.

I have one sister, Melissa, and two brothers, Reuben and William. Bespectacled Melissa was eleven months older than I — a fact she loved to flaunt before all our classmates at school. She also had short, curly, dark brown hair, while mine was thick, long, and black. Melissa's hair, however, never felt the heat of a straightening comb like mine did. Mama said that — Melissa's hair was a lot like grandma Stella's, while I took hair from daddy's side of the family.

My brother Reuben was short and stocky. He was also the comic in our family. I remember one time, he put a live goldfish in a bowl of tuna salad that mama had made for lunch. Afterwards, however, I don't believe Reuben thought his prank was so funny — not after mama placed a big scoop of tuna on his plate, and his happened to contain the gold fish. Reuben never tried that stunt again.

William and I, however, shared a very special bond — perhaps, because he was the oldest. Whenever I needed advice or directions, I could always go to William. William was also the one who helped me with my homework, gave me show fare from his part-time job earnings, and went to church with Melissa, Reuben, and I, each and every Sunday morning.

William was tall like our dad. But unlike dad, he had a very slender build. He took his creamy color from our mother and wore just a neatly trimmed, thin line of a mustache.

When William announced at the dinner table one

evening that he had enlisted in the Army that afternoon, none of us were surprised. It was just like him. William had always been helpful to the family and to anyone else, for that matter. Now, his country needed him.

I remember very well, how this news was received by the family. First, very quietly, mama got up, excused herself from the table, and went into her room . . . to pray. When she had gone, Dad got up slowly from his place at the head of the table, walked over to William, and gave him a big hug.

"William . . . William," I blurted. "I'll write you everyday . . . honest I will."

"I know. I know, Ruth Ann," William replied as he placed a gentle kiss on my forehead.

Reuben extended his glass of milk as if to give a toast and declared, "Here's to my big brother, William. The man who will end this war single-handed — as soon as he finds enough pebbles for his slingshot."

Reuben's remark brought laughter all around the dinner table.

A few weeks later, William packed his bag, and we all went down to the Grand Central Station to see him off. The station was crowded with soon-to-be soldier boys, some anxious, and some not so anxious, all going off to war. Amidst the noise of clanging bells and hissing steam, shoe-shine boys popped their rags to jigs, while mothers and young girls cried proudly and wished their soldier boys well. The conductor called out, the porters loaded the last of the bags, and my brother, William, was gone.

I still recall the first time William came home on leave. It was just after he had completed his six weeks of basic training. He looked so handsome in his uniform, and I felt proud as a peacock escorting him through the old neighborhood.

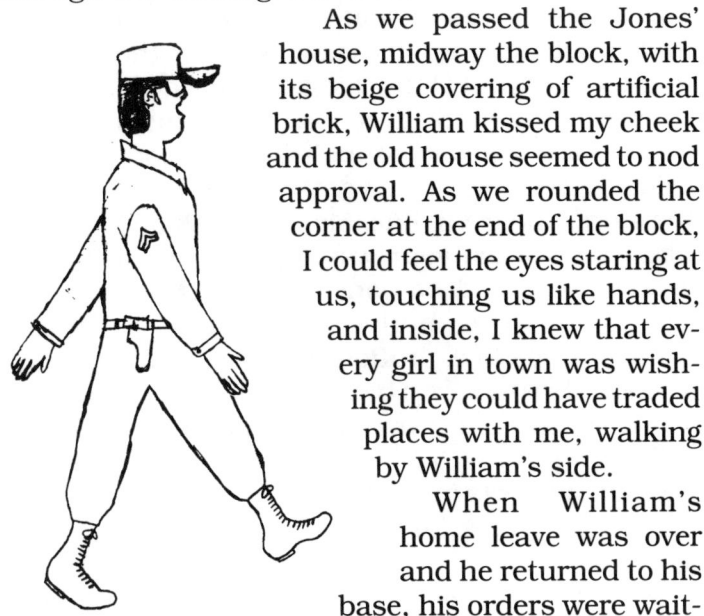

As we passed the Jones' house, midway the block, with its beige covering of artificial brick, William kissed my cheek and the old house seemed to nod approval. As we rounded the corner at the end of the block, I could feel the eyes staring at us, touching us like hands, and inside, I knew that every girl in town was wishing they could have traded places with me, walking by William's side.

When William's home leave was over and he returned to his base, his orders were waiting — *the South Pacific.*

I wrote William a letter each and every day, just as I had promised. As soon as Melissa and I came through the door from school, I'd dash into my bedroom and start my letter.

William wrote me back, but not on a daily basis. And reading one of his letters was almost like being there in the South Pacific jungle with him. He wrote about how malaria and other jungle diseases were taking a terrific toll on the men in his unit. Another enemy he mentioned was mud — thick and black. Sometimes, he wrote, they had to wade for miles in it, high as his knees, before reaching high ground. And all the time, snipers were firing all around.

On the home front, Americans across the nation had to deal with the rationing of commodities. Each family was issued a booklet of ration coupons on a monthly basis, and in a way, the coupons stated just how much of this or that a family could purchase. Still purchasing wasn't easy. Most of the time the markets were out of the things you needed most. And whenever the markets did get a shipment in, word would pass quickly through the neighborhood like wildfire. Everyone would grab their booklets, rush to the store, and get in line. More often than not, by the time you worked your way to the head of the line, everything would be gone. Mama use to say with frustration, "With butter, meat, sugar, coffee, and canned goods being rationed, how in the world am I supposed to prepare a balanced meal for this family."

At school, mock air raid drills replaced the fire drills. Everything, it seemed, had value, and many of the class projects involved collecting recyclable items like paper, grease, and metals.

One blustery and wintry day, as Melissa and I skipped through the snow on our way to school, Melissa paused. An angry frown came across her face as she turned to me and said, "Sure hope we don't have another mock air raid drill today."

"Why?" I asked, looking over at her.

"Well, that simpleton of a Charlie Smith tried to put his hand under my dress when that Air Warden turned out all the lights."

"Did you slap him?"

"You bet I did."

A sly smile came across Melissa's face as she pressed her cold face against mine and said, "Too bad, it wasn't that new boy, Steven Clark. I've been swooning over him."

"Oh, shut up," I snapped back. We both had a good laugh.

We skipped along in silence for a few minutes until I broke stride and said, "Melissa, how many War Saving Stamps have you pasted in your booklet?"

"Oh, its about half-full."

"Well, mine is all filled up. I'm going to turn it in today at school and purchase another War Saving Bond."

"You cheated. You must have cheated," Melissa screamed at me, "Where did you get the extra money, mama always gives us the same amount to buy War Saving Stamps with."

"Melissa, don't you remember the time I spent the weekend with Grandma Stella and Grandpa Luke?"

"Yes."

"Well, grandma Stella took me way upstairs in that musty smelling attic of hers and opened up a large cob webbed covered trunk . . . and Melissa, tucked inside that old trunk were all kinds of old treasures and junk like yellowed photographs, a moth ball smelling old army uniform of grandpa's, some high buttoned shoes, and about a dozen pair of — silk stockings."

"Silk stockings!" Melissa gasped as her mouth flew open. "Silk stockings. No one has silk stockings. They're high on the rationed list. Why all the young women around here wear nut-brown, leg make-up 'cause they just can't get silk stockings." Then, Melissa's voice modulated to a higher pitch as she asked, "Don't the government use silk to make parachutes with?"

"Every bit they can get," I replied sassily.

Frowning, Melissa pulled me close to her by one of my ears, and whispered, "Ruth Ann, I just know grandma Stella told you to split those silk stockings with me — didn't she?" Then, she pinched my ear hard before letting go.

I backed off a couple of steps to put some distance between us, then I stuck out my tongue and shot back, "Well, she didn't say so. Besides, I already sold them all at the Army Commissary — so there."

"How much did they pay you?" "All I'll say is that they paid me enough to fill my stamp book up . . . then some."

Melissa, by then, was furious. She reached down, scooped up two handfuls of snow, and let me have it — WHAM! As I wiped the dripping snow from my eyes, I noticed that I was right in front of the schoolhouse. Hurriedly, I ducked inside.

Still shaking and brushing the wet snow from my hair, I slowly turned the knob on the door of my sixth grade classroom. The bell had already rung, and bad boy, Charlie Smith, was up front leading the Pledge of Allegiance.

Quietly, I took off my coat and scarf, and hung them on the coat rack in the far corner of the room. All the time, I could feel the penetrating, hazel eyes of my teacher, Mrs. Bookspan, watching me, her blond hair combed straight back and done up in a bun on the back of her head. Self-consciously, I quietly scooted into my seat, fidgeting, as she walked up to the blackboard and began writing our assignments for the day.

Six weeks passed without a single word from William. I was worried. The whole family was worried. William had never gone that long without writing home before. Christmas was fast approaching. Yet, none of us felt any of the gaiety that was usually present, simply because — we had not heard from William.

Each day after school, and after having written my daily letter, I sat with my ears glued to the little radio on my night stand. I listened intently at what the broadcasters were saying, hoping desperately that they would mention something about the unit that William was fighting with. There was nothing. And when the paperboy delivered the paper each evening, I would hurriedly turn to the page where the names of the War casualties were listed. Praying silently, I would slowly read each name. I'd be so relieved when I couldn't find William's name listed there.

"Oh, why doesn't the President do something to end this horrible war," I use to scream to myself.

The next weekend, mama and I took the streetcar down town to shop. All the lamp posts along the route were sporting their Christmas outfits. Mama looked at me pensively and said, "Ruth Ann, this is one Christmas people on the home front will have a surplus of money to spend on gifts — with factory work being so plentiful."

Before I had time to answer her, a far away look flashed across her face, and she continued, "But, who feels like buying gifts when every family around here has a son or husband fighting in this horrible war."

Right away, I knew mama was thinking about William and the fact, that he would not be home for Christmas.

Another week passed, and still — not a word from William.

At dinner that evening, Benjamin, my dad, talked about buying a new home for the family. He said, he had saved enough money for a rather large down payment, and that he wanted a home with a spacious back yard and at least four roomy bedrooms. He also said, that he was certain that the better areas of the city would open up to Negroes — he was certain of that

While he and mama continued their conversation, I was daydreaming, wondering if he knew what he was talking about, and if he did, whether he would actually buy a house and move us there . . . and William — would he come home alive to enjoy the new house with us.

When dinner was over, I got up and went to my bed, but did not rest.

On the last day of school, before our Christmas vacation, Melissa and I walked slowly home from the old schoolhouse, side by side, pretending not to hear the constant churning noise of the presses and drills coming from the factory nearby. We passed snow covered houses, all standing neatly in a row with streams of light blue smoke from each of the chimneys framing an even bluer December sky that had patches of white clouds tacked here and there — mimicking a scene found only on carefully designed Christmas cards.

One neighbor, Mr. Foster, spotted us and waved as he pulled his Christmas tree behind on his son's wagon. We passed Reverend Johnson's house with its green and white shutters, and we waved to Mr. Finklestein as we passed Kahn's Department Store.

Finally, we arrived at our front door and the sweet smell of naphtha soap hit us as soon as we entered. "Mama's washing," we both said in unison. I took off my coat and rushed to the washroom where I found mama standing over her wringer-type washing machine. "Hi," I shouted over the washer's noise. "Did I get a letter today?"

Mama, did not answer.

Deciding not to bother her any further, I threw my

school books on an old day couch, hurried to the living room, and looked on top of our upright piano where the mail was usually kept. Expectantly, I stretched up on the tips of my toes and ran my hands back and forth across the top. I felt nothing. I was truly disappointed, hanging on the verge of tears. Suddenly, a familiar voice broke the silence.

"Ruth Ann," the voice said. "What are you looking for?"

I turned to see who it was, and screamed. It was William. "William," I shouted, "William. Oh, my God, you're home!" Instantly, I was choked with emotion and could not speak another word. Tears welled into my eyes and ran down hotly across my flushed cheeks.

William put his arms around me gently, and allowed me to sob all over his freshly starched uniform. When I had finished, he gave me his handkerchief which I used to blow my nose and dry away my tears of joy.

At that moment, Mama and Melissa came into the living room and explained that William would only be home for a few days — that he was on burial detail and was escorting the bodies of two soldiers from his unit — home.

My emotions on that day, this unusual homecoming day of my brother, William, was mixed with both sadness and joy, and it is something that I will never, never forget . . . . Never.

* * *

William survived the war, my father bought us a new house, and we spent many pleasurable years there.

Before I Wake

**by
Michael Nance**

As he slowly emerged from the dim reaches of a stupor induced by a large dose of a very potent opiate, Antoine saw in the shadows a blurred image of an anemic looking white man in a clerical collar. *Goddamn*, he thought, *a chaplain*.

Suddenly, the pain returned with a vengeance. The cancer, now in its last stages, had ravaged his body. He felt the familiar knifelike thrusts and could hardly ring for the nurse. A few moments later, an attractive, diminutive young Filipino woman glided past the chaplain who still stood in the doorway, but stepped aside, so that she could enter and administer the much needed relief.

As he watched her leave, he saw that the white cleric was still there, but looked even fuzzier. The drug had rapidly taken affect.

"Maybe, I should come back later," murmured the apparition-like figure.

Antoine settled back on his pillow. "Who asked you to come in the first place — ain't this a bitch?" Antoine said, his speech somewhat slurred, while his voice had a harsh bitter quality.

"Do you know . . . .," the white man groped for words, ". . . that Jesus came into the world to save sinners?"

"Look," said a tired and bored Antoine, "Marx said that religion was the 'opiate of the masses,' and since I can get all I need of the real thing by merely ringing for the nurse, I really don't need the brand you're dispensing."

The cleric was somewhat taken aback. He seemed surprised that Antoine had read Marx. And as he looked around the room, he was even more surprised to see on the table beside the bed, evidence that Antoine had, indeed, read Marx, the Rubaiyat, the King James Bible, the Koran, as well as Nietzsche and two fellows with French-sounding names which he had never heard, *Fanon* and *Cesaire*. He, therefore, decided to try another tactic.

"You read a lot I see."

"What's it to you?"

"It's just that, er . . . . Well, you seem to be an interesting person."

"Is that so?"

"Yes, and I thought we might communicate on an intellectual level."

"Really."

"Yes. Well, er . . . you know, before I entered divinity school I was a philosophy major."

"Where — Bob Jones University?"

"No. As a matter of fact, I attended a small liberal arts college in the Midwest. Before I found God, you see, I was something of an agnostic. I can't help but notice that despite your rather cynical attitude toward religion, you seem interested in the subject — judging from your choice of reading material. Are you, yourself, by chance an agnostic?"

Antoine caught his gaze. "Look, nothing you could possibly say, would interest me in the least. Will you please leave?"

"Okay, then," replied the cleric. "I'll come back later, if you wish."

"Go to hell," answered Antoine, "and let me be spared the commiseration of idiots." With that, Antoine closed his eyes and drifted off into a deep and troubled sleep . . . .

He was walking beside a boiling, putrid lake. The air was filled with voices calling out to him. "Antoine. Antoine," called a voice. It sounded like his mother's voice, distressed and plaintive. Then, a harsh, booming voice rang out, "Boy, you ain't shit. Never been shit, and never will be shit." That had to be his father. Then, there was Sandra's voice, almost a shriek, "You never loved me, never loved me, never loved me. You sonofabitch!"

He awoke suddenly, bathed in sweat, and beheld with alarm, the tired grizzled face of his father whom he had not seen in ten long years. He was so surprised that he shook himself, although it was extremely painful, trying to make sure he was actually awake. It was no dream. His father was, indeed, at his bedside. They looked deeply into each other's eyes — long, silent, searching looks. Antoine finally broke the silence.

"I never thought I'd see you again, this side of hell."

The old man looked hurt. "I came, didn't I?"

"Yeah, you came."

"If I had ever thought you needed me, or even wanted to see me, I would have come before."

"Really? I always thought you hated me. I thought you never wanted to see me again. Do you remember what you told me in the other hospital, ten years ago, right in front of my mother? You said, 'Nothing from nothing, leaves nothing.'"

"Well, shit. You had . . ."

"Does that matter? No, you never forgive and forget. That's your code, isn't it?"

"Look, I came after all these years. I came, didn't I?"

"Yeah," Antoine said wearily. "You did come. But why — why, now?"

"Because I'm your father. Because you're my son. My only son."

"Are you sure? I heard you had others."

"You're the only one I claimed."

"Besides, when you left the hospital ten years ago, I figured that you had always hated me — ever since I was in my mother's womb. I guess I was that bitter. But then, when I was a child, I always thought you loved me. I didn't know a lot of things. I didn't know that you never loved my mother — that you only married her because she was pregnant with me, and you always worried about what people would think. I didn't know then, that at the time you married my mother, that you were in love with that other woman — the one that destroyed herself because you didn't marry her."

"What the fuck do you know about that? You weren't there. What do you know? You always think you know so much. You read all these goddamn books. If you like to read so much, why didn't you ever finish school? Why have you never been anything but a bum? Liquor. Drugs. You wouldn't even work. Writing all that shit. It never made you any money."

"Yeah, I know. There's no substitute for it, is there?"

"I never found any. But, tha . . .," the old man's speech faltered. "That's not what I came here for. I wanted to see you because you're my son, and, and . . ."

"I'm dying of cancer. so, you felt guilty and . . ."

"Shut up. What do you know about life? All you know is books. You never knew anything about life. I loved your mother when I married her. I loved you. But, you're so twisted inside that you can't understand."

Antoine's eyes filled with tears. He told himself that it was from the terrible pain that was wracking his body. And yet, he knew that he always wanted his father's acceptance, his father's love. He had thought he would never see him again. But, here he was, at his deathbed. That must prove something. With some effort, he reached over and gripped his father's hand — gripped it as hard as he could. A strange smile crossed his face, and suddenly, he fell back on his pillow — dead.

* * *

The Washtenaw Incident

by
Michael Bernard Tolliver

It was not the five a.m. darkness that frightened him on this particular Friday morning. Melvin Williams traveled this route to work daily, leaving his brightly lit Ann Arbor, Michigan complex, entering the blackness of Clark Road, then cutting through Washtenaw Community College. And no, it wasn't the severity of the day's fog, that promoted his childhood fear. It was something else. Something that he could not see or touch or hear. Something else. Something that gripped him with icy fingers, sent chills racing up and down his spine, and caused him to grip the steering wheel so tight that his joints ached with pain.

"No!," he yelled out into the darkness. "This ain't no drive-in movie. Dracula, werewolf, and killer tomatoes are kid's shit. Ain't Real. What am I — a kid?" He laughed at his silliness. "If I told Bobby about this he'd laugh his ass off after all that agent orange, jungle warfare, and V.C., we seen."

Bobby Manchester and Melvin had been friends for many years, even lived in the same apartment building, visiting each other regularly, listening to music, and exchanging time worn war stories. Bobby's stories, however, were usually centered around tales of death and drug use — the latter being his favorite. He also worked at Washtenaw Community College in the chemical laboratory, where he often concocted his own dope.

Melvin looked to his right and into the surrounding forest where the eyes of small creatures glowed faintly like tiny earthbound stars. Acknowledging that the eyes were probably small animals eased some of the tension, so did switching on the jazz station where Nancy Wilson moaned "Mr. Bojangles."

"Jam, JZZ. Sing nice to me, Nancy," he said as he hummed along with the tune.

As he rounded a curve, he was greeted by a pair of larger yellowish dots glowing in the dark. "What the hell," he said as he pumped the brakes with his right foot, while pressing on his bright lights with his left. The dots quickly transformed into a distinguishable pair of eyes. He slowed his car slightly, then came to a complete stop. There before him, chewing on a melon in the middle of the road was an enormous raccoon, the largest he had ever seen.

He blew his horn and raced his engine, but the raccoon did not move. And, instead of being frightened, the bright lights seemed only to serve as a dining light for the beast. "Just my luck to tear up my ride on a — a-what? A damn big-ass raccoon. Move. Move, you hairy bandit. You're making me late for work!" He blew the car horn several times more, but the racoon only glanced up and continued to gnaw at its melon.

"Well, alright. You bad. I'll just plow your dumb ass under! Goodbye, muther. Here I come!" He stepped heavy on the gas and the car jumped forward like Flo-Jo off the starting blocks in the hundred meters.

At the last second, the creature turned and scooted into the forest just before the car splattered the melon into nothingness. Melvin chuckled.

Turning the radio up a bit, Melvin released a sigh of relief and drove on to the beat of Grover Washington Jr.'s "Inner City Blues." Randy Crawford's rendition of "Imagine," carried him to his Livonia auto plant.

Despite the extraordinary amount of work required trying to help his department catch up on their weekly production goals, he just could not forget the size of the raccoon he had encountered that morning — *One big mother-fucker.*

After work, he collected his weekly pay check and drove to the Ann Arbor Bank and Trust where he saw his friend Bobby in the parking lot.

"Hey, Bobby! What's shaking?" he shouted. "Yeah, I see you runnin' to get that eagle air bound. Stop by for a drink or something tonight. Got to tell you something."

"Sounds good to me," Bobby said as he rushed to get inside the bank doors before closing time. "I'll bring the — or something — knowing you ain't got the stuff I want. Be there about nine or ten . . . . Between nine and ten," he repeated.

That night before the door bell could complete its ring, Melvin opened the door quickly without a hello. "Bobby," he said with excitement. "You won't believe the size of the coon I saw running around your place this morning. Man it was . . ."

"The hell I won't," Bobby broke in. "Big as a shepherd?"

"How do you know?"

"We were breeding it in the lab. Got away Thursday night."

"You mean, you all made that thing?"

"Yes. You going to let me in, Melvin? Or, are you going to discuss all of Washtenaw Community's business out here in the doorway? I need to sit, pour, sip, and fill my nose. Then, I'll update you on my world of lab tech's fun and games!"

"Sure, Bobby. You ain't in yet? Courvoisier, rocks?" Melvin asked as he walked toward his kitchen. "Close and lock my door behind you, then sit, and get ready to explain."

"Great, while you get my drink, I'll just get myself real ready," Bobby answered as he reached in his pocket and placed a small envelope on the dining room table. "Bring me a plate, Melvin," he yelled. "Want to make this a little finer powder. Goes up the nose better that way. Hey! Want to try some of this, man?"

"In one word, no! In two, Hell no! And before you start getting high on that lab-made shit of yours, you gonna tell me how the lab made that raccoon, or not?" Melvin said as he reentered from the kitchen. "Here's your plate, your Courvoisier, and your rocks! George Jefferson, can the maid get you anything else — sir?"

"This isn't Thursday. Your off day is gone the way of high button shoes. How dare you act so uppity," Bobby said using his pocket knife as a holder to sniff the powder. "This is some mean shit here. Here man, try it. This shit is even better than that opium-laced weed we had in the Nam."

"This ain't the Nam, Bobby. I don't fool with that now. The raccoon — tell me about the fucking coon! Talk while I play some Miles for you."

While waiting anxiously for Bobby to start talking, Melvin walked over to his tape player, placed "The Man with the Horn" in the slot, and pressed all the buttons necessary to fill the room with music.

"Well, only a few people at the lab know about it." Bobby took another snort of the lab-made dope. "We found this raccoon — a little, hungry, puny looking mother and injected it with some experimental muscle building and body enlarging chemicals — more as a

118

prank than anything else. Then, the coon started growing, almost overnight. Before long, he was big as a fucking dog, and that ain't no lie. By then, we discovered that the coon had turned into a real junkie. Loved the stuff to no end.

Several times we tried to wean him off, but the damn thing would go into a rage. So, we kept feeding it to him to keep him quiet. Wasn't no big thing. The top bosses don't know the time of day, anyway. Then, this shit-head coon breaks out of this cage we had him in, and got away. Now, the damn thing's running free, and the only thing he'll eat is melons and that lab shit we made. That ass is as strung-out as me. Now, we got a pool going. Fifty apiece, and there's ten of us. All we got to do is bait a few traps, and when he comes to chow down, we gun him down. Two- fifty for you, two-fifty for me. Be like old times. Me, you, weapons, the bush, killing. Lord knows I miss the Nam. I got no business in this world. If it wasn't for my dope, I couldn't cope. Hey, cope with dope," Bobby emphasized with a spaced out grin.

"Yes, you're right. Only a dope would try to cope on dope. And where do you get this 'we' shit? Old times? I don't need no old times. In the Nam, we were the hunters, as well as the hunted. But now, if you're asking me to help kill this big ass coon for two-fifty, then I'm your man. We talking about a shot in the head, and dead, right? Nothing more, nothing less — just nod your head in between your dope snorts, if you agree."

"I cope on dope," Bobby said holding his head back and stuffing his nose again. "That's the deal, ain't nothing real. We waste the mother-fucker, then pick up our money — green cash. Five in the morning, going to get my uncle's coon dog from Detroit. Be back to get you at seven. Then — we kick ass."

Bobby used his fingers to wipe up the last of his dope and licked his fingers. Then, he leaned back in his chair and nodded off into a drug induced coma.

Somewhat reluctantly, Melvin went to his closet and took out a deer rifle from the spot it had been resting in since the day Bobby gave it to him as a present, hoping to stir his interest in hunting. Then, he got his cleaning materials and sat at the table to clean his weapon, something he used to do nightly in Nam while listening to the Armed Forces Radio Network and praying that he would survive. He never asked for more — just one day at a time. He was one of the lucky ones. His strategy had worked and he made it back. Still, there was a price. For although he had been back in the world for several years now, he was never able to totally forget Nam, its stinking hot jungles, or the blood of his friend who had died in his arms. There was always something that kept reminding him — something that took the liberty of crowding into his dreams, and turning them into nightmares. *Fuck the Nam.*

"Where the hell you get that AK-47, and what's that machete for?" Melvin asked Bobby with a real concern. "What are we after out here — V.C. or a fucking coon?"

"Just a little extra fire power, Mel. Get those two traps out the back of the car."

"It ain't the firepower that bothers me. You straight enough to be firing that thing? I don't want no holes in my ass!"

"Shut your face!" Bobby yelled as he grabbed the leash on the dog and walked away. "I can blast the spots off a ladybug's ass at fifty paces from the hip."

"Well, you just keep that muther pointed down

range and away from me." Quickly, Melvin took the traps from the car trunk and hurried to catch Bobby, still wondering why Bobby thought it was necessary to bring an AK-47 and a damn machete like the ones they wore hanging from their belts in Nam.

The morning cool had burned off by the time the men had baited their traps with lab-dope, and started to stalk their prey with the canine in the lead. After several hours of following the frisky, sniffing hound, the dog led them back near the area where they had set their second trap. Sure enough, there was the raccoon feeding voraciously beneath a nearby bush with one leg still held fast in the trap. The trap's anchor chain, however, had been broken.

"See Mel," Bobby whispered as he extinguished a rolled joint of his home-grown marijuana. "I told you — the sonofabitch loves that shit we cooked up in the lab. It's in the bush now.

"I'll send the dog in to smoke him out. Be ready." The mutt dashed into the bush. The raccoon turned to run, but found that the trap was hindering his progress. He stopped then, faced the dog, and backed off until he was cornered near the stump of a tree, staring wildly as the mutt barked to signal his job — well done.

Melvin and Bobby, both shouted with glee as they raced through the brush to finish the job. Suddenly, the snarling raccoon leaped, catching the dog by surprise. A vicious fight followed. The dog danced in and out, and succeeded in biting the raccoon several times. But the dog was no match for the superior muscle mass of the raccoon. Within seconds, the coon had the dog's jugular vein in a vise-like grip between its sharp teeth, sending its teeth even deeper. The mutt howled in pain.

Melvin arrived on the scene several paces ahead of Bobby, fired at the coon and missed. Before he could fire a second shot, the coon released the dog and scurried away into the undergrowth.

Both men ran to the spot where the whining dog lay. Blood spurted from the open wound about its neck, and it was plain to see that the dog was mortally wounded. Solemnly, Bobby pointed his AK-47 at the animal's head.

"Sorry I got you in this mess, boy," he said as he closed his eyes and fired one round, point blank, into the dog's head. The dog whined no more.

"An eye for a fucking eye," Bobby said in rage as he shoved a fresh clip of ammo into his AK-47. "It's killing time! They kill one of yours, goddamnit, you kill ten of them!"

Melvin looking at Bobby, watched as Bobby removed a bandanna from his pocket and tied it around his head like a sweat band. For a split second, he was back in Nam, listening to the same pep talk, trying to get himself emotionally prepared for another patrol through the insect infested jungle, wading waist high through rice paddies, and poking into well camouflaged tunnels and bunkers, and . . .

"Time to kick ass!" Bobby shouted, moving quickly to follow the bloodstained trail of the raccoon.

Somewhat apprehensively, Melvin followed. "Hey, Bobby, slow down." Melvin yelled. "This ain't the fucking Nam. This is Ann Arbor, Michigan."

Bobby, however, was out of hearing range. So, Melvin slowed his pace to a leisurely walk. *Something's wrong. This shit ain't going down right*, he said to himself.

Twenty minutes later, Bobby spotted the raccoon lying on its side panting for air at the edge of a clearing. "I got you now. Your bad ass is mine, you ugly mother."

Cautiously, he pointed his AK-47 at the animal and crept closer. Ten feet, then five. At five, he lowered his weapon and took the machete from his belt. "Shooting's too good for you — sonofabitch. I'm going to hack you up just like you did my uncle's dog. Eye for eye. You scared? You gon' die, mother-fucker. Ain't you scared?"

Suddenly his voice was drowned out by a deep threatening growl as the raccoon sprang from its resting place and leaped straight for his throat. Bobby feinted to one side and drove the point of his machete straight into the animal's heart. The raccoon fell to the ground, dead.

Then, something happened, something strange and unexpected. Bobby threw his machete to the ground and started firing blindly into the forest, screaming and crying all at the same time, "It's killing time. Little, fuck ass, tunnel rats. It's killing time . . . killing time!"

That's what was happening when Melvin raced into the clearing to see what was going on. Suddenly, he stopped dead in his tracks. He knew the signs. Bobby had gone off and this wasn't the time to intrude. So, he froze and waited until Bobby had emptied his clip, but even then, Bobby was still pulling the trigger and crying softly.

"Bobby," he said.

Bobby turned around quickly, pointed the empty gun in his direction, and snapped the trigger.

"Cool it, Bobby," Melvin said as he dropped for cover. "It's me, Melvin, goddamnit."

Bobby looked at him through glazed eyes. Slowly, he seemed to recognize him, so Melvin released a long, hard sigh of relief. Slowly, Bobby lowered the gun, turned, and looked down into the cold eyes of the dying animal. Suddenly, for no apparent reason, his body started shaking like a single leaf in a chilling wind.

With some concern, Melvin walked up to Bobby and placed his hand gently on his shoulder. Bobby jumped in fear.

"Shit. What the hell you doing, Melvin? Get the fuck away from me, you goddamn coward. What did you kill — what do you know about killing? Not shit. If it hadn't been for me, you would probably still be over there pushing up jungle flowers."

"It ain't that, Bobby. I just want to leave the Nam in Nam. Fuck all this killing."

Bobby and Melvin didn't speak for three days although they saw each other in passing almost daily.

In the meantime, Bobby collected the five hundred dollars from his co-workers, took the racoon home, removed the fat and soaked it in vinegar for a day. Then, he placed the raccoon — head, tail and all, on a pit of fire. When the raccoon had cooked, he sliced the head, wrapped it separately, and placed it in the refrigerator with the rest of the carcass.

On the fourth day, Bobby's phone rang. He answered it. It was Melvin.

"Hello, Bobby. It's me, Melvin."

"Yeah, Mel?"

"Didn't want much. Just called to see if you're still alive."

"Look, Mel. Man, I'm sorry about the way things went down — you know, just . . . just one of them things."

"Hey, man, don't tell me. I understand what's happening."

"Mel, you don't understand shit. You can't understand. No one can understand unless they have been there with me — to the same place at the same time."

"Well, I guess you right. We been friends a long time. Been through some heavy shit. You know me, I'll follow you anywhere. But man, I don't want to go with you on your dope trips. I can't. That lab dope fucks up your mind. One day, you gon' get out there so far, you can't get back. Seriously, Bobby, maybe you ought to see one of them specialists at the V. A. hospital or something. Maybe, they can help. It's worth a try."

"Yeah, maybe I'll do that — maybe I won't. Look, man I got your part of the bounty money — two hundred and fifty dollars, just like I said."

"Well get it out! I could sure use it."

"Well, won't you come over and pick it up tonight. We can drink some juice, talk a little shit, and listen to some sounds."

"Okay, be there about eight."

That night, the two men sipped cognac on the rocks, enjoying each other and a friendship that had survived for some fifteen years. Brook Benton's "Rainy Night in Georgia," filtered softly in the background.

"You remember that tune, Bobby?" Melvin asked.

"Every time it rains, Melvin. Say, how you like this cognac?"

"This is good stuff, man. What kind is it?"

"The best kind, Mel. The best kind. Ain't no label 'cause I mixed two or three together. Might even bottle it up and sell it."

"Well, whatever it is — it's the best I've ever drank. Listening to Rainy Night in Georgia, kind of reminds you of the Nam, don't it? Us sitting out by a campfire drinking beer after a mission, and Top Sarge cussing like a sailor, looking for us to clean latrines."

"Yeah, that red-neck had to be crazy — thinking I was going to hang around emptying shit after crawling on my ass through jungle all day."

"To this day, he still don't know where our hideout was. Man, that used to piss that red-neck off."

Both men chuckled, then laid back in peace. Brook Benton sang on.

* * *

"Wake up, Cherry. Off your ass, on your fucking feet. We got some ass to kick today. Briefing in ten minutes."

Melvin rolled over and looked into the grim, camouflaged face of his Team Leader, Corporal Bobby Manchester. Quickly, he jumped out the sack, dressed, put on his war paint, grabbed his M-16, and rushed to the briefing tent.

Their mission was a "Search and Destroy," to be accomplished in two man teams. S-2 had located an area that contained a network of numerous tunnels. Their job was to search them out, clear them, collect any information available, and then, destroy the tunnels. When the briefing was over, Corporal Manchester pulled him to the side.

"Well, Cherry. Today you get your first experience killing tunnel rats. You follow me, do exactly as I say, and I'll get your ass back alive. By the way, where you from in the world?"

"Detroit."

"No shit. Put it there, homeboy. I come from Ann Arbor. In the bush, I'm in command! Anywhere else, use my first name — corporal. You digging what I'm saying?"

"Sure, Bobby . . ., I mean, yes, commander."

"You learning fast, son. That's good."

Three hours later, they were still stalking tensely through the humid jungle, quietly probing, and listening. Another hour passed before Bobby, who was in the front, gave him the clenched fist signal. He stopped where he was, his heart rate suddenly on the increase. Bobby had spotted something.

Bobby approached a clump of undergrowth cautiously from the side, watching the ground carefully, looking for signs of trip wires and booby traps. Then, he stopped and gave me the signal to follow in his footsteps.

When Melvin was along side, Bobby pulled the pin of a concussion grenade, pitched it into the hole and waited for the ear shattering explosion. When the dust settled, the two waited for signs of life or movement. There were none.

"One of us got to go in," Bobby said with a John Wayne smirk.

Melvin swallowed hard.

"Don't worry, I'll show you how it's done, homeboy. Piece of cake."

While Melvin stood guard, Bobby fired several quick bursts into the tunnel, then disappeared into its depths.

After what appeared to be a lifetime, Bobby emerged suddenly, startling Melvin.

"Nothing in there, homeboy. Nil," Bobby said shaking his head. "S-2 is full of shit. Tell you what. We'll check out one more, claim we checked out a dozen, then head back for the checkpoint and wait for Sarge. And when we get back, I'll treat you to a beer with a cherry and some of the best weed this side of Heaven."

"The only thing I want is the other half of my round trip ticket back to the world."

"Well, you stick with me and I'll teach you how to

survive and stay alive. And it ain't in no training manual. The fucking manual'll get your ass killed."

"What was it like down there?"

"Take a look for yourself."

"Maybe the next one."

"The next one may kill you. Now get your ass in the hole and check it out. How in the hell you're going to learn to fight this war? Second handed?"

Melvin grabbed the flashlight from Bobby's hand apprehensively, then lowered himself in the pitch black hole. The smell of marijuana was thick. To ease his childhood fears that reminded him of horror movies, he hummed tunes by the Temptations. "Farewell My Love," was his exit song.

"One more tunnel," Bobby said as he took the point.

Melvin followed close, but not too close. Within a hour, they had discovered their second tunnel. Bobby gave the signal and they both dropped to their knees. While Melvin covered the entrance, Bobby stalked to within target distance of the entrance and pulled the pin of his grenade. His arm was starting its arc, when suddenly a large beast from hell lunged from the entrance with an unearthly growl, striking Bobby with a force that sent him crashing to the ground.

Melvin saw the grenade sailing in his direction. Instinctively, he turned and dove for cover as the grenade exploded around him. He was shaken badly. He turned to check on Bobby and screamed in terror as he watched an unholy creature possessed of a body that resembled a saber toothed tiger and the grotesque head of a raccoon standing over Bobby's unconscious body, his bloody mouth ripping viciously into the flesh of his throat.

"Mother-fucker," he shouted to the top of his lungs. The beast turned and charged. He scrambled for his weapon, threw it on automatic, and fired wildly at the charging animal, striking him several times. Still, the beast came. He emptied his clip. He reached for another one. Almost had it in when the beast leaped. The last thing he saw were angry yellow eyes and a pair of huge, gleaming white, dagger-like teeth.

"Angel Dust" by Gil Scott Heron and Brian Jackson had played all night before a neighbor finally called the police to complain about the noise. It was still playing when the police forced open the apartment door and found the bodies of two young men — both dead, their faces etched in fear.

The one identified as Melvin Williams was lying in an overturned easy chair. The other, a Bobby Manchester, was lying flat across the sofa, his hands clutching his throat.

No marks were found on either of the bodies. There was no sign of a struggle or disturbance. The Inspector did find a bottle of liquor. He gave that to forensic and told them to have it analyzed.

Later, the coroner ruled that the deaths were caused by heart failure induced by an overdose of a very potent and heretofore, unknown drug.

* * *

Peeping Jane

by
Barbara Hunter

Saturday finally arrived, bright and sunny, the air slightly crisp. It was only 10:30 a.m. Yet for some reason, it appeared to be much later. Maybe, because there were so many people out on the street.

Miles Banard Wellings — a young man sitting on top of the world. A recent graduate from law school, Miles passed his bar examination, then went to work for the prestigious law firm of Targon, Winston, Singleton, and Huff. The world held no boundaries for him.

I was introduced to Miles during the staff party for the new members of the firm where I also worked. Shortly afterwards, we became pretty good friends.

One mid-morning, Miles, a couple of colleagues, and I were brunching together, discussing various issues, and enjoying our meal. Mine was especially enjoyable, since I had been forced to sit through a dreaded dinner which was lovingly prepared by my lady friend on the previous night — one that made my stomach run for cover, and almost made me swear off food for good.

Suddenly, Miles said quite loudly, "Who is — she!"

Well, needless to say we were all quite astonished by the sudden interruption of our legal conversation — the effect of which was like some inquiring soul knocking on the bathroom door while one was engaged in deep contemplation.

We all looked first at Miles, then in the direction

of his hypnotized gaze. Confusion filled our faces as we observed the lady in question, trying to understand what about her had provoked such a response. I decided his eyesight was on the wane, so I offered him my carrot juice.

Miles ignored me, got up, walked over to the lady's table boldly, and said something to her. When he returned, it was quite obvious that he had been rejected. I thought his psyche couldn't take it. His pride was clearly wounded.

"Well, what's all the fuss about?" I asked, still unable to understand why a young man who had pinup quality girls chasing after him would be interested in Bree.

"I can't believe it," Miles stated. "I asked her for a date and she turned me down. This is the first time this has ever happened to me."

"Forget it, Miles. Bree's not your type, anyway. Frankly, I'm amazed that you're even interested in her."

"Bree? Do you know her?"

"Well, sort of."

"Come on, man, let's hear it."

"Her name is Bree Beatrice Jane Goodwin. Works as a counselor for emotionally troubled youths. She's single. Doesn't have a boyfriend — you know, in between engagements. She's intelligent, blind as a bat without her glasses or contacts and defensive as heck about it, too. She smokes a little too much, eats a little too much, and has the personality to win the soul of the devil. Anything else you want to know?" I added with a chuckle.

"Where does she live?"

"That, I don't know, but her receptionist, Norma, lives next door to my lady friend, Helen."

"Preston," Miles asked with urgency, "you and

Helen have got to do me a favor so I can find out more about this woman."

"Like what?"

"Get your Helen to set up a card game. Invite me and this Norma over to play, so I can pick her brains."

"Well . . ., I don't know, Miles. I . . ."

"Please, Preston, you've got to."

"Well, okay," I agreed even though I still had some misgivings.

The next day, I made the suggestion to my girlfriend. She didn't care for Miles, and naturally, she didn't like the idea.

"I don't like it one bit," she said in anger. "Miles is just on another one of his ego stroking adventures, and he is doing it at our expense. What he wants us to do is to help set up his kill for him. I wish you would learn to keep your mouth shut. One of these days, I'm going to tie one end of a rope around your tongue and the other to the bumper of a damn bus!"

I said nothing. I just let her get everything off her chest. When she finished, she finally agreed with some reluctance, and with the understanding that we just out right tell Norma what Miles had in mind.

* * *

Two nights later, we were all sitting at the card table in Helen's living room waiting for Miles to get there. While Helen went to the kitchen to get some more snacks, I explained the situation to Norma.

"Well, Preston," Norma said, smiling suggestively as she lifted her stocking clad foot beneath the table, shoved it between my thighs, and caressed my crotch intimately with the tips of her toes, "so there's finally something you want from me."

I smiled sheepishly and managed to nod, "Yes," just before I went into a coughing fit, hoping Helen had not observed the interplay between us. It wasn't that I disliked Norma. She had made these types of advances before. But she and Helen were friends, and I knew that what she had in mind was dangerous. Otherwise, I would have been in her pants long, long before now.

At that moment, the door bell rang and Helen went to answer it. It was Miles. I made the introductions, and Miles and Helen took their seats at the table. "So what you want to know about Bree?" Norma asked quite bluntly before the game could get started.

Her question caught Miles off guard, but he recovered quickly and said, "Any and everything you can tell me."

"Well, it's going to cost. Ain't nothing free these days and certainly not information."

"Name your price," Miles stated as he leaned back in his chair.

"For a start, I want two tickets to the Luther Vandross concert."

"That's easy enough."

"Then, I want lunch delivered to my job for three days — with a dozen roses."

"Roses?"

"Absolutely — one dozen. Then, I want you to arrange a date for me with one of your good-looking colleagues. Any problems with that?"

"No," Miles agreed to Norma's exorbitant demands and my mouth dropped.

Immediately, the card game was forgotten. Helen and I sat twiddling our thumbs, while Miles and Norma spent the rest of the night discussing Bree.

From that moment on, the guy began to act like he was campaigning for a political office or something, sending flowers to Bree's home and her place of work, writing her sweet notes attached to 8 x 10 pictures of himself, and numerous invitations to dinner — all to no avail.

In the meantime, he continued to pester Norma for more information. We were all having drinks after work one evening when Norma lost her patience and shouted quite sarcastically, "Has it crossed your mind, Mr. Slick, that you're using the wrong approach?" Then, she grabbed her purse and stalked out.

The loss of Norma as a ready source of information, however, did not deter Miles. Somehow, he discovered Bree's favorite Friday lunch spot, and his campaign shifted into a new gear.

"Come on, Preston," Miles demanded. "We are having lunch at the Purple Tree today."

"Why the Purple Tree?" I asked.

"You'll see," he replied.

We arrived at the Purple Tree thirty minutes before the lunch crowd. Immediately, Miles found the head waiter and gave him fifty dollars with instructions to escort Bree to his table when she arrived.

As soon as I realized what he was about, I begged off. "Look Miles, I'd rather not be here when Bree arrives. If it's alright with you, I'll just have my lunch at the bar. I don't even want to be near when the shit hits the fan."

Miles agreed reluctantly, and I left for the bar. I had hardly sat down, when Bree walked into the door. The head waiter saw her, too, and escorted her to Mile's table. I could see the confused look on her face as she looked at the waiter and glanced around for another table. After a short moment, she sighed, sat down, ignored Miles, and ordered fried rice with shrimp.

Undaunted, Miles attempted to engage in a conversation, or should I say a monologue, talking in soft tones, while Bree looked at him in total disgust.

What key word, words, or phrases Miles employed to ultimately gain Bree's attention is still a mystery to this day. But after a few moments, time seemed to pause, and in that span of time, I watched as something strange happened — Bree's impenetrable, bellicose facade disintegrated right before my very eyes. Her eyes drooped seductively. Her lips glowed invitingly like a moist piece of freshly sliced pineapple. Her face flushed and toned.

Curiosity nudged me violently, so I got up and slowly made my way to a table near them so that I could hear what was going down.

"Mr. Wellings," Bree said as she lit a cigarette and crossed a nervous right leg over her left. "You are the most persistent, pompous, egotistical man I have ever been exposed to. So, tell me, Mr. Wellings, what is it exactly, that you want?'

"Alright," Miles said, trying to make eye contact through the smoky cloud of Bree's cigarette. "All I want to do is get to know you better."

"Why? And why me?"

"Well . . ., I know this is qoing to sound strange, but . . . well . . ."

"But what?"

"I think I'm in love with you," Miles blurted out, and I almost choked on my drink.

"Are you nuts — or what?"

"Frankly, I don't know if I'm nuts or not. I am filled with mixed feelings of confusion. You look and act like you don't want to be bothered. And yet, on the other hand, I see you haven't left."

"Maybe, I should," Bree stated with a smirking mouth. "Number one—you don't even know me, and number two—you are not the only man on this earth. That means, I do have a choice."

"Now let me tell you something. I am not questioning your right to a choice. All I'm asking is that you give me a fair chance. I find you a very interesting person. I want to get to know you. It's as simple as that. Nothing more. Nothing less. Is that so difficult to believe?"

"Yes, it is," Bree stated with fear in her eyes. "I have been burned badly once, and scorched several times. Men like you remind me of a smoldering volcano, one of nature's wonders — something to be viewed from far afield."

"You have my sympathy, but not my condolences. You are an extremely lovely lady, and you're not the only one who has been burned in a relationship. It happens everyday. I understand your reservation, and if you would like to terminate this conversation and leave . . . well, I can understand that, too. If not, might I suggest that we begin again—my name is Miles Banard Wellings."

For a moment, Bree sat silently, indecision written clearly on her face. Suddenly, she smiled softly and said with a degree of warmth unknown to me, "I am pleased to meet you, sir. My name is Bree Beatrice Jane Goodwin."

I couldn't help it. I suddenly laughed aloud in joy. Miles looked at me, gave me the finger (or thumbs up), and smiled. Then, he turned to Bree and said, "Beautiful lady, shall we adjoin for a quieter place to continue our conversation—somewhere far away from my nosey friend over there?"

"Why certainly, Mr. Wellings," Bree replied with mock haughtiness as she looked at me and smiled.

I stood up and held my glass aloft in tribute to them as Miles took Bree by the arm and ushered her to the door — all five-feet-four inches of her *two-hundred and sixty-five pound mass. Truly, amazing*, I said to myself.

* * *

Lance Courage

**by
Harry M. Anderson**

Sunday morning came. The streets of Detroit were quiet and Lance was very restless. He had woke up about 3 a.m., paced the floor, then lay back down on his bed. A short time later, he was up again.

At 6 a.m., Lance showered, dressed, and went to breakfast at the Elias Brother's Big Boy restaurant in the Renaissance Center. He ate light, his elbows resting on the table, his mind preoccupied with the upcoming race. He was a Lotus driver and the race scheduled for that day was important to him, not because it was a Grand Prix race or just another stop along its circuit. It was the Detroit Grand Prix. Detroit—the Motor City. The only American stop on the circuit.

He finished his breakfast and went up to his room to change into his racing overalls. The moment he had waited for was almost there.

When he left his room and entered the lobby at 7:30 a.m., his girlfriend, Penny was waiting. She was dressed in a white and yellow striped blouse, white slacks, yellow stockings, and white huaraches. She walked up to him and placed a gentle kiss on his cheek, the delightful scent of her Avon perfume heavy in the morning air.

"How's my champ this morning?"

"He's okay, for the time being," Lance replied as he and Penny walked out the door toward the circuit.

"Good. You give 'em hell, baby. I'll be in the stands cheering for you all the way."

"Thanks, Penny. I'll need it today, baby."

When they reached the grand stand, Penny stopped and pulled Lance close. "Well. good luck, Lancelot, my love," she whispered, kissed his cheek again, and headed for the stands.

When Penny had gone, Lance sighed and continued to the circuit to prepare for the half hour warm up session scheduled for 9 a.m.

It was a beautiful, sunny day with the temperature in the upper 80's and no forecast for rain — an ideal day for a race. All along the circuit, American flags were on display, and riding over the deep rumble of revving engines were the excited voices of the multitudes of people who had turned out for the Detroit Grand Prix — blacks, whites, Hispanics, affluent middle-classers, teenagers, young adults, and middle-aged and senior citizens. Lance knew they were there, and although he derived a certain satisfaction in that fact, he knew that he would have to block them out of his mind in order to concentrate on the race.

As Lance approached the pit area, several of his fans rushed to get his autograph. He politely signed a few, but did not tarry.

When he arrived, his Lotus crew was setting up the open-wheel racer he was to drive in today's race. He nodded to them, then climbed upon the pit wall and sat near his Number 11, Lotus 10IT, quietly, still in deep meditation and still deeply concerned. Marshall, a crew member, walked over to Lance and leaned against the wall.

"How's it going, eh?"

"Okay, I guess."

"I can tell you have a lot on your mind. Make sure your car's all set during the practice session and let us know how things are when you're on the track—if the car is race ready."

Lance gave him the "thumbs up" signal.

The untimed practice session went on without a hitch. The Lotus was letter perfect with good braking, handling, and power. For tires, however, Lance decided to run on the not-so-hard, not-so-soft "B" compound Goodyear Eagle Radials. So, he had the crew put them on while the SCCA sanctioned Sports Renault race was in progress.

While the crew worked, Lance took a seat on the ground behind the pit wall and closed his eyes, ignoring the noise and preparing his mind for the task at hand. Nothing else mattered, not the crowd, not his parents and relatives who were in attendance, nor Penny, his dearly beloved—only the race, the biggest race in his career. A race that could put him in strong contention for the World Championship. All he had to do was — *win.*

Soon it was 12:45 p.m. Thirty minutes and counting.

A little anxious, Lance dropped his Bell helmet over his head and strapped on his Cosworth-powered Lotus. When he was settled, he gave a thumb and the crew pushed him out of the pit to the starting grid. In front of him, on the pole, was Ellis in a Ferrari. Next to him was Marcel Francois in a BMW V-6 powered Brabham. In the second row was Franz Faulhaber in a McLaren Honda V-10, third on the grid. The Irishman, Mark O'Malley was fourth in the Renault-powered Williams. In the third row, the Englishman, Steve McGuinn, in a Benetton-Cosworth, fifth on the grid. Then came Lance, sixth on the grid.

All about the racers, the crew members shouted

last minute instructions and made their final mechanical adjustments.

Marshall said something to one of the crew members, wiped his hands, and walked over to Lance. "Go get 'em, eh!" Marshall said as he leaned over Lance's cockpit. "You can do it. The crowd's behind you. Make 'em happy."

Lance took a quick glance up at the stands. They were filled to their 85,000 capacity. Ten thousand more than expected. Suddenly, over the public address system, he heard the Governor of the State give the famous call:

"GENTLEMEN . . . START YOUR ENGINES!"

The crowd roared to its feet as the small, 3.5 litre engines came to life in a melee of spurting thunder. Seconds later, millions of balloons climbed into the sky high above the Motor City while the crews scurried back to their respective pit areas.

The cheers from the crowd drowned out the roar of the engines as the racers pulled off to pace themselves around the 2.5 mile street circuit in the warm-up lap.

When the warm-up lap was completed, the cars were again gridded for the start. Behind the wheel, Lance felt his heart beating faster. *25 seconds* . . . His blood flow gained momentum. *20 seconds* . . . The pupils of his eyes closed into slits like those of a caged tiger. *15 seconds* . . . He could feel the effects of the increased adrenalin . . . *10 seconds* . . . and the strength of his muscular system felt ten times stronger as he gripped the wheel and gearshift knob. *5 seconds* . . . Sweat ran down his body and suddenly, the green flag dropped, and the green light flashed — green. The Detroit Grand Prix was on!

Lance got a good jump on McGuinn in the Benetton, and he was running fifth when the field screamed into the left-hand curve onto the Atwater straight. Ellis, in the Ferrari, set a blistering pace as he led the field down the long Atwater straightaway. Marcel, in the Brabham, was only three-tenths of a second behind.

Shooting into the sharp right-hander near the Promenade Level, they charged up the straightaway into the quick right-hander at Woodbridge Avenue. The top six were: Ellis (Ferrari), Francois (Brabham-BMW), Faulhaber (McLaren-Honda), O'Malley (Williams-Renault), Lance (Lotus-Ford), and McGuinn (Benetton-Cosworth).

As the field roared down the Chrysler Service drive past the Crain Communications Building, they went into a left-hand turn onto Congress Avenue. A good place, Lance decided, to make his move on O'Malley who was dropping off the pace of Ellis, Francois, and Faulhaber. Lance pulled alongside the Williams-Renault as they charged down Congress Avenue. He measured his distance. When the moment felt right, he turned up the boost and jumped past the Renault-powered racer just before the quick left at the Congress-Beaubien intersection which was followed by a right-hand turn onto Larned. *One down,* he said to himself grimly as he darted under the tunnel of the Millender Center and zipped down Larned at 155 miles per hour.

Ahead, he spotted the red and white rear wing of Faulhaber's McLaren. The gap was slowly closing. Then he lost sight of it and concentrated on gearing down and braking heavily into the left-hander onto the short Woodward straight that ran pass the City-County Building and the statue of the "Spirit of Detroit."

When Lance came out of the right-hand turn onto the Jefferson Avenue service drive, he stood up on the accelerator, hitting 146 miles per hour before he was forced to gear down and brake for the tight left turn around Cobo Hall. He crossed the trolley tracks and swept down the ramp, completing a right-hander, which led him down the short straight into a battle for fourth place.

The McLaren and the Lotus made the sharp left together as they passed the Lansdowne Restaurant and dove into the Goodyear Tunnel. But as they came out, each forgot about the other and concentrated on breaking through the very tight right and left-handers near the Renaissance Center. Swinging out of the last turn, Franz Faulhaber and Lance charged down the short straight into the chicane, then darted across the start/finish line.

Not unlike the races at both Monaco and Zolder, the two staged a battle between them which was a crowd pleaser, dogging each other, and staying within striking distance of Marcel in the Brabham. Up front, however, Ellis had built up a 12 second lead over the field in his Ferrari.

For the next ten laps, Lance and Faulhaber battled. On the 11th lap, Lance got lucky and passed him on the Larned straightaway. He was now running third, 13.4 seconds behind Marcel, and 25 seconds behind Ellis.

On lap 21, Lance opened up a gap of 24.2 seconds on Faulhaber. In the meantime, Marcel, who had lost ground on Ellis, suddenly found a spurt of power in his BMW V-6, and by lap 26, the Frenchman was only a car length behind the Ferrari.

The crowd went wild as the battle continued for the next 16 laps.

With Ellis struggling to hold off Marcel, Lance was holding his own — running third, unchallenged. His confidence surged as he heard the encouraging roars of the Motor City crowd who waved their American flags wildly, and zestfully. On lap 42, Marcel started to have gearbox trouble. At Congress Avenue, he lost fourth gear. The Ferrari pulled away. Marcel fell off pace and allowed his vehicle to coast from Beaubien to Larned. At Larned, Marcel saw Lance's Lotus coming up in his rear view mirror. In order to prevent an accident, he raised his right arm to alert Lance that he was pulling off to the right to let him by.

With Marcel out of the way, Lance put the pedal to metal and the Lotus leaped with renewed vigor, speeding by Marcel as the Frenchman drifted into the runoff area at the Woodward-Larned intersection and unstrapped himself from the cockpit. For Marcel Francois, the Detroit Grand Prix was finished in 42 laps, thanks to a broken gearbox.

Ellis, however, was still enjoying a comfortable lead with Lance running second—doing all he could to catch the fleeing Ferrari. Guido Narducci, in the Minardi, was a distant third.

Hans Von Schmidt continued to make a spectacular showing for the Detroit crowd by working his way to fifth place behind Luigi Minardi in the Osella-Alfa Romeo.

Lance continued his attack, applying the pressure to Ellis, gaining and average of two seconds per lap. Ten laps later, he had reduced the Ferrari pilot's 42 second lead to 20.3 seconds, and the crowd was in complete bedlam as they cheered Lance on in his chase to catch the Englishman.

By the 52nd lap, the Detroit street course had taken a severe toll, and there were only 11 cars out of 26 still running. The standings were: 1. Ellis (Ferrari); 2. Lance (Lotus); 3. Narducci (Minardi); 4. Von Schmidt (Lotus); 5. Minardi (Osella); 6. Elford (Tyrrel); 7. Guerrero (Brabham); 8. Salazar (Brabham);

9. Bianchi (Ferrari); 10. Thompson (Arrows); and 11 — Redman (Williams).

The cheers, "GO! GO! GO!" drowned out the sound of the engines as Lance steadily closed in on Ellis. Somewhere in the back of his mind, he could hear the voice of Bruce Springsteen singing "Born in the USA," his rallying tune, and one that never failed to egg him on.

By lap 55 the gap between him and the Ferrari was down to 17.5 seconds. Suddenly, to Lance's surprise, the Ferrari leaped and gained three more seconds, quickly. Lance realized then, that Ellis still had an abundance of reserve power at his disposal and his chances of catching him were turning bleak. That being the case, Lance decided to concentrate on maintaining his spot as second.

On lap 58, just five laps from the finish, while Ellis was charging down Jefferson, a huge cloud of smoke and steam suddenly billowed out of the rear end of his Ferrari. Lance recognized the signs immediately—a blown engine. Ellis had lost his air, turbo, and water pressure, and he could see the Englishman cursing and frantically banging his fist in frustration as he coasted down the Jefferson Avenue service drive into the runoff area at Jefferson and Washington Boulevard. The Englishman got out and watched Lance cruise by Cobo Hall.

Ellis's misfortune put Lance out in front, with Narducci second, and Hans now running third. He thundered through the Motor City with a small smile and one thought in his mind — *It ain't over, 'til it's over!*

On the final lap he came charging out of the Goodyear Tunnel with full confidence—*Two more turns and a chicane.*

When Lance swept through the chicane, he spotted the checkered flag fluttering in the wind daringly, and the closer he approached, the louder the words of Bruce Springsteen's "Born in the USA" came in his mind.

No, it ain't over, 'til it's over he said to himself again as he crossed the hallowed finish line.

Behind him, Narducci finished second, and Hans took a spectacular third after starting 16th on the grid.

On his cool-down lap, Lance spotted the arm of a corner marshall holding out an American Flag. He grabbed it and continued his victory lap, holding the medium-sized flag high in the wind with his left hand, and searching the nameless faces for someone he recognized — like Penny.

By then, the crowd was in total chaos, cheering wildly, dancing, and singing with pride — all paying tribute to a black youngster from an old and humble origin, who had just won — the Detroit Grand Prix!

* * *

Hard Times

by
Herbert R. Metoyer, Jr.

Oakdale is a small, rural, Creole community nestled in the heart of Central Louisiana. The yard of almost every home was adorned with beautiful magnolia trees, and during the summer the fragrance of their large, brilliant-white flowers would blend with that of the honeysuckles which grew wild on vines along the dusty streets and from every back yard fence.

We lived in the black section of town on the opposite side of the railroad tracks in an area commonly referred to by all as the *Quarters*.

Oakdale was typical of many small, Southern towns in the 1930s. While we boasted a few teachers and an abundance of preachers, most of the inhabitants earned a meager living as servants, mill workers, or peddlers who passed through the Quarters twice a day — each with their own special, and sometimes colorful chants which were spoken with a mixture of English and Creole. During the summer, the peddlers sold such items as crawfish, milk, eggs, blackberries, sugar cane, melons, snap beans, tomatoes, and other garden produce. During the winter months, they sold fire wood, fish, and wild game.

My father was more fortunate and he was able to get a job at the local sawmill where he worked as a laborer earning fifteen to eighteen dollars a week. Out of this sum came expenses for the house payment, food, clothing, and wood for the stove. What was left went for miscellaneous expenses such as church donations, ice for our ice box, and last, but not least, *burial insurance*.

Burial insurance was similar to life insurance as we know it today. They were small policies with a face value of no more than one to two-hundred dollars — just enough to cover the cost of one's burial, and of course, no self respecting citizen would dare be caught dead without one.

My parents had two such policies, one for each, that was sold to them by a white *Cajun* that we all called "Frenchy, the Insurance Man."

Frenchy was typical of most Cajuns, those trapped between two worlds, unwilling to accept the new, and equally unwilling to release the old. Most of the time, Frenchy wore a cane-woven straw hat, especially during the summer, and overalls with a starched, white shirt and a bright green tie which he never tied. He walked with a slight limp that many of the neighborhood children, and myself, found amusing until my mother told us that he had been wounded during the First World War. From that moment on, we looked at Frenchy from a new perspective, and he became more of a celebrity instead of an object of ridicule.

Despite his handicap, Frenchy was an extremely friendly person who usually had a kind word for everyone. He, however, did tend to get a little testy whenever he encountered difficulties in collecting his weekly insurance premiums. In those cases, more likely than not, he would give his customers an impromptu lecture about how they should manage their budgets in order to satisfy their obligations.

Paydays for all occupations occurred like clockwork every friday evening—creating an air of excitement and anticipation throughout the Quarters. The lonesome wail of the sawmill's whistle promptly at five o'clock would mark its place in time for the whole town. Supper would be cooked early and wives would sit on their steps, sometimes in groups, laughing and gossiping, and waiting for their men to come home with their weekly earnings. And while they were so occupied, old man Joe Edwards would sit beneath the shade of his favorite persimmon tree and strum his ancient steel guitar.

My mother's favorite spot was in the swing mounted on our *galerie*. The evening shade from the china-ball tree in our front yard made it ideal. From there, she had a clear view of the Sante Fe railway and the direction from which my father always came. My sister, Delores, was a toddler, and while our mother relaxed in the swing, she and I would play in the front yard behind the security of our once white, in need of paint, picket fence.

When my father turned the corner, my mother would announce his arrival, and we would race to meet him at the gate. He would lay his bicycle aside, pick us up, and nuzzle our necks playfully with his day old beard while we squealed, covered our necks with our hands, and dodged his canine growling antics. Even today, with little effort, I can close my eyes and imagine the odor of the pine and hickory sawdust mixed with that of sweat and Bull Durham chewing tobacco that permeated his coarse overalls.

That evening, grocery bills would be tallied and paid, and debts between friends—settled. Children would get *Lagniappes*, penny candies or cookies from the storekeeper, while our parents received extra measures of fatback, red beans, or rice.

Much later — there would be an increase in activity at the "Blue Hall," a popular, local juke joint. Drinking and dancing took place in the front half of the two story, boxlike structure, while *drinking* and gambling took place in the rear. The revelry and the heavy, *gut bucket* blues bass beat of the jukebox would last long into the night, and I would lay awake, looking out the window, watching the dazzling display of the lightning bugs, fighting sleep, and yet, waiting — for it to come and conquer me.

Every Tuesday following payday, Frenchy would pass through the Quarters, house to house, collecting his weekly insurance premiums.
"*Bonjour — Comment ca va?*"
"*Comme si, comme sa,* (so, so)," was my mother's usual reply.
"You got you gon' be dead money, todey — Ruby?" Frenchy would ask while wiping the sweat from his sun-reddened face on the sleeve of his already wet shirt.
In our case, the premium was twenty cents a week for the two policies. Frenchy would collect the money, make an illegible notation in his school-paper notebook, then proceed to the next house — his *chapeau de paille* (straw hat) bouncing in syncopation with his short, choppy stride.

One week, for several days, there were some mechanical difficulties at the saw mill and my father could not work. The men, however, were still required to report and remain on site each day until the repairs were completed — all without pay. As a result, this unexpected shortage of funds threw my parents already unmanageable budget into total chaos.
When Frenchy came by the following Tuesday, my mother explained the problem and stated that — although she did not have the money then, she would try and catch up the following week — "Lord willin'."

The second week came and we were still no better off. Again, she informed Frenchy that she would try to have it by the next week, for sure . . . "If the Lord be willin'."

When the third week arrived, however, we were worse off than before and my mother was too embarrassed to tell Frenchy again that she did not have the money. Besides, she now needed sixty cents.

So, to relieve herself of this situation, she instructed me to tell Frenchy when he came that she was not home. I was a little over three years old then, but followed instructions very well.

While she watched for his approach from her bedroom window, I played marbles on her freshly, lye scrubbed, wood floor, enjoying its honeysuckle odor and the sight of its clean, bleached-white expanse. As Frenchy approached, she rushed back into the living room and quickly repeated her instructions, "Now, when the insurance man knocks, you open the door, and tell him . . . My-mother-is-not-home." Well . . . that seemed simple enough.

She then positioned me at the door where I waited — poised. As soon as Frenchy knocked, I jerked open the door and shouted as loud as I could, "My mother's not home."

"*Salleau prie!* (Doggonit)," Frenchy said as he slapped the side of his thigh with his notebook heavily. I jumped. "Well — where you *Maman* done gone at?"

Without hesitation, I replied, "Behind the door."

From the look on Frenchy's face, I knew immediately that something had gone wrong. My suspicions were confirmed when the big hands of my mother lifted me by the scuff of my neck, and with a back-hand flip, sent me skidding across the floor in a wild

151

bouncing turn. Shamed, she apologized to Frenchy humbly.

"Dat's a good thin', you sorrie —what you done do lak dat. Dat's one no-for-good, dirty trick — having that little boy lie lak you done did."

"I know it wasn't right, Mr. Frenchy. I just don't have the money yet."

"Payday — whot you do? Dey sawmill been sawing for most two weeks, now. What you do—take you money and go buy a new dress or somethin'?"

"No sir, Mr. Frenchy—haven't bought a new dress for more than two years . . . . Just seems like every penny I get — goes down a black hole or something."

"Well, whot you gon' do? Dat's no good — you gon' die and all wid no 'sorrance for you graveyard digging."

"Next week, Mr. Frenchy. I'll have it for sure next week — Lord willin'."

"Well Ruby, I know hard times done been stomping your corns, but he done went his way and gone now. And the mo' longer you wait, the mo' you gon' owe. Now, you fix you head so you don't forgot to pay next week when I gon' come back. *Bonsoir*."

"*Bonsoir*, Mr. Frenchy."

My mother picked me up and we stood in the doorway swaying side to side as Frenchy left and proceeded to the next house. Tears swelled in the corners of her eyes, then ran down the chubby cheeks of her beautiful face, fell to her breasts, and melted the starch in her homemade, gingham dress. I didn't understand why, but suddenly, I felt very sad, too. My mother later told me — that at that moment, she was promising God that she would never teach a child to lie again.

My baby sister, who had been asleep, started to

cry. She put me down then, and we went to attend her.

The next week, it seems the Lord was still not willin', and our financial situation was worse. And the closer Tuesday approached, the more depressed my mother became.

Finally, the dreaded day arrived. The morning sun found her up early, preparing herself for the inevitable. Outside while the chickadees and redbirds chattered, my father left and joined the line of men passing on their way to the mill, their syrup-bucket lunch cans pinging brightly against the metal buttons of their well worn, denim overalls.

With deliberate care, my mother cleaned our house, put on a fresh starched dress, combed her hair, and powdered her face like she did each Sunday morning before we went to church. Afterwards, she spent the rest of the morning preparing and steeling herself emotionally for the task at hand, singing *Trees* and trying to decide the nicest way to tell Frenchy that she still did not have the money.

Again, she watched from her bedroom window, her face set and intense. Before long, I heard her talking to herself, and the more she talked the angrier she grew. ". . . and who does he think he is, anyway? Always waving that raggedy paper in my face, like his insurance is the only bill I've got to pay. Hear him tell, you'd swear I was dying tomorrow . . . . Here, I can't even buy myself a descent pair of drawers, eating fatback and grits, and him hollering about dying money. Crackers don't give a damn about nobody but themselves — must think I'm a fool. I'll pay him when I'm good and ready, and if he can't wait until I'm good and ready — he can take his ole insurance policiee and shove it where the sun don't shine!"

On and on, she ranted. I had never seen her so angry before — not even the time she chased my father out the house and stood on the front porch throwing every biscuit we had down the street after him. She was truly angry then, but that was nothing compared to her anger on this day.

Suddenly, her raving stopped and I knew instinctively that Frenchy was coming down the street. In silence, she got up, bristled, took a deep breath, and started stoutly toward the door. I waited wild eyed and expectantly. My mother was a big woman and I truly feared for Frenchy's life. But then, at the last moment, just before Frenchy knocked—my mother suddenly turned, grabbed me and my sister, and we dashed out the back door and into our *Cabane* (outhouse) where we hid.

As we sat and waited, I peered down into the black depths of one of the holes, trying to see past the maggots and soiled newspapers, and wondering if these were the "black holes" my mother often referred to—the ones where all our money went. In our solitude, we could hear Frenchy knocking loudly at our front door.

Finally, Frenchy got tired and went away. When we were sure that he was gone, my mother released a sigh of relief, and we went walking way down by the school house, my sister in her arms, and me — trailing close behind.

My mother said, she wasn't "Stut'in 'bout Frenchy," and we didn't even try to get back home until it was way past supper-time.

* * *

Author's Biographies

by
Dianne White Morris

Dianne White Morris —Dianne is the secretary for the Detroit Black Writers' Guild. She is a native Detroiter and the mother of one son, Daniel. She attended Northern and MacKenzie High Schools.

Dianne enjoys reading and writing, and although she has written numerous short stories and poems, her first love is writing inspirational stories for children.

Dianne would like to dedicate her entry, "A Father for Malik," to her husband, Matthew, for all the patience and support he has given her. Dianne also served as one of the editors for this book.

Ruth Rosa Green — Ruth Rosa Green, a retired elementary school teacher and administrator, was born in Piqua, Ohio. She was raised and educated in Ohio and Michigan, receiving her Bachelor of Science degree from Wilberforce University in Wilberforce, Ohio, and her Masters of Education degree from Wayne State University in Detroit.

Ruth, a widow, resides in Southfield, Michigan. She's the mother of three daughters and one son, and has seven grandchildren. Ruth became an avid reader and lover of poetry at an early age. Her writings began in 1935 and has continued, intermittently, throughout her life.

Her first book of poetry, *Insights and Expressions,* was published in 1985, and her second book of poetry and short stories, *Thro' My Mind's Eye*, was published in 1989.

While Ruth continues to write poetry and short stories, she is also working on a historical-biographical book about the West Eight Mile Road area of Detroit during its pioneering days. Hopefully, it will be published in the near future.

Lafayette L. King — Lafayette resides in Detroit, and works for a temporary agency as a word processor. He started writing stories in elementary school as part of his school assignments. After having written thousands of letters to track and keep in touch with family members, Lafayette decided to pursue writing as a hobby.

He joined the Black Writers' Guild in 1984. He is an avid reader and writer who firmly believes that writing should be an essential part of everyone's life.

Mr. King served as one of the editors who was instrumental in publication of this book.

Suma (Melanie Lyn Rios-Nance) — has been writing since 1982. The fact that Melanie is legally blind and suffering from the vagaries of a schizophrenia-related illness, has not hampered her in the pursuit of her life's goals and ambitions. A member of Schizophrenic Anonymous, she has gone public to expound upon the issue of advocacy. She is also a member of the Worker's World Party, and has dedicated her life to fighting for the rights of the disabled and the unemployed.

Melanie loves to write, especially on subjects related to the health field. She and her husband, Michael Nance (author of the title story) are the proud parents of one son, Angelo Miguel Antonio, age five.

Michael Nance — was born in Detroit, Michigan, October 4, 1948. He graduated from Central High and attended Wayne State University. He has been writing off and on for the past twenty-five years, and has been published by the *Black Conscience, Inner City Voice, Solid Ground, and Nostalgia for the Present.*

Over the years, Michael has written several short stories, numerous poems, and a one-act play. He enjoys jazz, and reads all genres of literature. The classics, however, are his favorite.

Barbara L. Hunter — was born in Ann Arbor, Michigan, and raised in Kalamazoo, Michigan. At the age of fourteen, she started her education on the streets of Detroit, searching for her identity. Despite the hardships, this new world of the big city served as her inspiration and provided the fertile ground from which she garnered an incessant desire to write.

At the present time, Barbara is a widow with three children and works as a laboratory technician. Her aspiration, however, is to become a salaried, self sustaining writer. Erotic literature is her forte.

Harry M. Anderson — was born August 17, 1959. He attended Wayne State University where he obtained a Liberal Arts Degree in Journalism. Currently, Harry is a freelance sports writer for Detroit area publications. He has also written articles for the *South End* (Wayne State University), *Oakland Press, Windsor Star, Michigan Chronicle,* and several other smaller newspapers.

Harry is also writing a sports related novel which he hopes to see published soon.

Michael Bernard Tolliver — was born October 16, 1947 in Hamtramck, Michigan, graduating from Mackenzie High School in 1966. From 1966 to 1970, he served in the United States Air Force and spent one year in Thailand in support of the Vietnam war effort. Afterwards, he attended and graduated from the Control Data Institute.

Michael is primarily a poet with over fifty poems to his credit. Some of his work was published by this guild in *Through Ebony Eyes*. The story contained herein is his first attempt at short story writing. He is also working on a novel.

Peggy A. Moore — a native Detroiter, is probably one of our most active members. She is the founder and director of the *Detroit Black Writers' Guild*. Peggy is a special woman with a wide vision who formed the guild in an effort to increase literacy awareness among inner city residents and to provide a medium for publishing their efforts. She is also author of a book titled *How Not to Abuse Your Child*. She also holds workshops dealing with the problems of early childhood, and is the publisher of the *Westside Journal*. Peggy — is special.

Robert K. Jones — was born in Detroit in 1937 when the west side of the city was an area of corn fields and small livestock pens. He is a graduate of Wayne State University where he was the editor of their award winning Engineering Magazine. Currently, Bob works as a supervisor in the Ford Motor Company's Research and Engineering Center.

Bob has been writing short stories now for twenty years. When he is not writing, he dabbles in his other hobbies, art and astronomy. He and his wife, Joe Ann

Whitworth, are the parents of two sons, Matthew and Kimani. Look for a novel by Bob in the near future which will recreate the saga of the west side during the late 40s and early 50s.

Herbert R. Metoyer — is a retired military officer and helicopter pilot who now works with General Motors as an engineer in their Body Test Laboratory. He was born in Louisiana and attended undergraduate school at Southern University where he obtained a B.S. Degree in Liberal Arts and a commission of 2nd lieutenant in the United States Army.

Herb is a published poet, folk singer, and songwriter. In 1966, he recorded an album on MGM's Verve-Folkways label. One of his songs went international and another, recorded by another artist, was selected by the astronauts to be included in the time capsule which was placed on the moon.

In 1968, he was selected as one of three poets honored by the State of North Carolina's Arts Council.

Beyond the above, most of Herb's writing has been of a technical nature associated with his duties as an Aeronautical Engineer in the military and as a Mechanical Engineer with General Motors. He, however, has great expectations and is looking forward to a very rewarding career as a writer of historical fiction.

* * *